THE ATHEIST

THE DEIFORM FELLOWSHIP ONE

SARAH ETTRITCH

NORN PUBLISHING

TORONTO, CANADA

ISBN 978-1-927369-06-7

Editing by Marg Gilks

v1

Published by Norn Publishing
www.NornPublishing.com

For Kath and Jim

Acknowledgements

My thanks to Jennifer Brinkman (my lovely partner and wonderful beta reader) and Marg Gilks (my fabulous editor).

Chapter One

Jillian slid her ID card through the reader and waited for the security system to confirm her identity. The opaque door swung open. Diana beamed as Jillian walked past her desk. "Good morning, Agent Campbell. He's expecting you."

"Good morning," Jillian said curtly, her eyes drawn to Diana's perfect smile. The woman should be starring in toothpaste commercials, not pushing paper and fetching coffee. As for Keller, he'd better be expecting her, considering the bastard had called her in two days early. She knocked on his door and pushed it open without waiting for an invitation to enter.

Keller shifted the phone receiver to his left hand and pressed it against his ear. "Yeah," he said, glancing at Jillian and gesturing toward one of the empty chairs in front of his desk. "I get where you're coming from, but it'll have to wait until next week."

Ignoring the chairs, Jillian folded her arms and gazed out the nearest window.

"I know, I know, but it's the best I can do."

Her chest tightened. She rocked on her heels.

"Look, I have to go. I've got you down for Tuesday at ten, okay? Yeah, send it to me." The receiver went down. "Jillian, I'm sorry." She turned in time to see him round his desk, wringing his hands. "I know you're supposed to be off. Can Diana get you something? Coffee?"

"I don't drink coffee."

"Right," he mumbled. "Well, sit down."

"What's this about? It sounded urgent."

"Sit down, sit down," he said, settling back into his chair.

With a quiet sigh, she sank into one of the chairs and flicked a piece of lint off her jeans. "Well?"

Resting his elbows on his desk, he gave her an anemic smile. "I know you've only just completed an assignment—"

"Don't tell me you want me to go under again?" she said, wincing at the eagerness in her voice. He'd agreed to at least a month of desk duty.

"I don't, but—"

"I'm supposed to be taking a break. Wait—what do you mean, *you* don't, but?"

Keller grimaced. "It's Donaldson . . ."

"Donaldson?" Her voice sounded shrill. *Calm down.* "What does Donaldson have to do with it?" she asked levelly.

"He asked for you . . . as a favour."

"Tell him no," she said firmly.

"I can't, not after I squeezed him for three of his agents last year. I knew he'd call it in at some point." Keller's fingers found a pen, which found its way to his mouth. He chewed on its end.

Poor Keller, having to suffer through the discomfort of asking me to work for Donaldson. Pardon me for not being sympathetic. He'd have forgotten about it by lunchtime. Conscious of the open office door, she lowered her voice. "I am the worst person he could ask for. You know that, Keller."

"He's read your file. He's aware of your history."

Her history—what a quaint way to put it. "Then why is he asking for *me*? He could ask for anyone. Why me?"

He met her eyes. "Because you're good. And I got the impression that something big is going down."

She quirked a brow. "You don't know what it's about?"

"Need to know only," he replied. "And apparently, I don't."

What could Donaldson be working on that was so confidential? His team worked the conspiracy and religion cases, for Pete's sake. His agents spent most of their time investigating dinky websites thrown up by fanatical teenagers seized by the Holy flipping Spirit or whatever they were calling it these days. *Beware the antichrist! 666!* and all that crap, next to a photo of some two-bit politician. Did Donaldson's agents ever go undercover when investigating the nut case of the week? She hadn't thought so. Few agents could pass for fourteen.

"I wouldn't ask if it wasn't important." A moment's pause. "About fifteen minutes before Donaldson called me, I saw Hudson in his office."

The pieces fell into place.

"There has to be a connection," Keller said.

There was, between Keller wanting to impress Director Hudson so he could snag that promotion he'd wanted for years, and Keller leaning on her to do something he damn-well knew she wouldn't want to do.

"It won't just do wonders for me. It'll do wonders for you, too," Keller said, his eyes shrewd. "You obviously came up during their little tête-à-tête. They want you. You love working undercover, so why not?"

She did love working undercover; it was easier being someone else. But lately there seemed less of herself to return to after an operation. It had frightened her after the last one, how uncomfortable she'd felt to be back in her own skin, and how unsettling it was to gaze in the mirror and see a stranger. She felt like an intruder in her own apartment, seeing her things, but not her things. Hobbies she'd long abandoned. A mother and stepfather she hardly saw. No friends, unless you counted the guy behind the counter at the local pizza joint.

The psychologist—mandatory after every operation—had suggested that Jillian not go undercover for three months. Keller had balked, and Jillian hadn't fought him too hard. While she'd known deep down that a time-out might do her good, the idea had also scared the crap out of her, and three months had sounded like an eternity. They'd compromised, and with the psychologist's approval, had agreed to a month's break, followed by a re-evaluation. "Andrews won't agree to it."

"Andrews will agree to whatever Hudson wants," Keller said with a dismissive wave of his hand. "Come on, Jillian, it's not as if you had a breakdown, right? Andrews only raised desk duty because you hinted at it. And I bet you're regretting that now, aren't you?" His grin was too wide. "If it wasn't Donaldson, I bet you'd be jumping at it, Andrews be damned."

She cursed his perceptiveness. Would she go crazy behind a desk? What would she do with herself every night? She wiped clammy hands on her jeans.

Keller leaned over his desk. "Just talk to him," he said smoothly. "You can always say no."

Could she, with Hudson involved?

"You're here . . ."

"All right, all right!" If she didn't hear Donaldson out, Keller would never forgive her.

He rolled back his chair and sprang to his feet. "Let's go," he said, motioning impatiently for her to stand up. When she did, he took her elbow.

"Don't worry, I won't make a run for it," she said. "But no promises," she warned as they walked to Donaldson's office. "If I don't like what I hear . . ."

Keller shrugged. "That'll be on you, not me. The moment you're in his office, my part in this is complete."

Jillian wanted to shake her head at the most honest words to come out of Keller's mouth since she'd arrived.

Keller rapped on Donaldson's open office door. Donaldson looked up from the file on his desk and peered at them through his glasses. "Agent Campbell," Keller said.

"Good." Donaldson flipped the file closed. "Come in and shut the door behind you."

She turned to Keller to murmur a good-bye, but he'd already set off down the corridor, relieved to be out of it, no doubt. After closing the door, she faced Donaldson, hoping her indifference didn't show.

"Please, have a seat. May I call you Jill?"

"It's Jillian," she snapped.

"I'm sorry. Jillian. And I'm Donald."

She coughed into her hand as she sat down. Donald Donaldson? Who would name their kid Donald Donaldson? Amused eyes studied her. He was probably used to her reaction to his name. She almost grinned at him, then remembered which department he headed. "Agent Keller said you're interested in working with me."

He leaned back in his chair and formed a steeple with his fingers. "I thought of it more as you working for me."

She crossed her legs. "I'm supposed to be going on desk duty for a while."

"Yet you're here. Do the job right, and you'll be on desk duty soon enough."

"What's the job?"

Donaldson pressed a button on his desk's control panel. A man's face appeared on the flat screen mounted on the west wall. "Jim Preston. Reverend Jim Preston. Runs a makeshift church in the financial district. Offers services during lunch hour. He and his church are becoming quite popular, especially with those from the nearby financial institutions and companies."

Jillian relaxed. Donaldson had probably asked for her because she normally went undercover for white-collar crime cases. "So what's the problem? Some nut's giving inspirational talks while people eat the lunch they grabbed from the local food court. Hardly cause for alarm."

"We believe he'll entice people to invest large amounts of money into his organization. He's already started a fundraising campaign to raise money for a soup kitchen, and there's talk about buying a building."

She snorted. "Since when did churches raising large amounts of money for themselves become a crime?"

"In this case, we believe he'll collect the money and run," Donaldson said with a frown.

As far as Jillian was concerned, it would serve the gullible donors right.

"Also, several executives attend his services. Preston preaches some pretty radical ideas about sharing wealth, capping salaries—"

"Don't tell me you're worried that his ideas will infect those hardened executives and capitalism will fall on its ass? They're attending to find out what he's saying, so they can laugh about it back in the office."

Donaldson chuckled. "Our concern is that companies will invest in Preston's scheme for PR purposes, especially through donation matching. Corporations might be able to absorb the loss of a few thousand dollars, but what about their employees? Plus, if Preston gets away with it here, he'll do it again in another city."

Jillian folded her arms. "Where do I come in?"

"We need someone to get close to Preston and find evidence that he's a fraud, that he's planning to abscond with the donations."

"Use whoever gathered the information you already know." Someone must have scoped out the services and reported back.

"My agents don't go undercover. Yes, one of us attended a couple of services, but anyone can note who's there and read a fundraising flyer. We need someone to get close to Preston and gain his trust, someone who'll arrive at his services seeking enlightenment, who'll not only sit at his feet, but make herself useful, so she'll be invited into his circle of trusted confidantes."

Her stomach knotted. "No. Find someone else."

"Preston's church is interdenominational. Like many of his ilk, he's drawn from numerous religions and created a mishmash philosophy. It's not a Christian—"

"Does he mention God? You keep calling it a church, so he must."

"Yes, he—"

"No." Jillian shot up from her chair. "I'm not doing it."

"Look, I know you're skeptical—"

"Skeptical? I don't believe it. It's bunk. I can't do it."

Donaldson's face tightened. "You pretend to be someone you aren't all the time."

"I pretend to be a top-notch accountant, so I can get my hands on a company's internal financials. I become best friends with the boss and his worker bees. I listen in on gossip when everyone's blotto." Jillian jabbed a finger at Donaldson. "What you're asking me to do will be too much of a stretch."

They glared at each other. Jillian wanted to take a deep breath to slow her breathing, but she would *not* show any sign of weakness. Unfortunately, neither would he. "I normally don't go undercover here. I live here," Jillian said desperately.

Donaldson shrugged. "You run into someone, you stick to your cover. Don't invite anyone associated with Preston home."

As if she would.

"Your family and friends all think you work for a bank, anyway. Right?"

Her family did. She didn't have to worry about all her non-existent friends.

"You're the best agent for the case," he said quietly, still staring at her. "You'll fit in with the financial crowd. You speak the language—both languages."

"I haven't stepped foot inside a church since I left home. I don't know the language."

"Yes, you do."

Why was he being so persistent? Couldn't he see her agitation while merely discussing it? What did he think would happen when she walked into that "church?" Didn't he understand that she wouldn't be convincing, that she might even blow her cover? At this point, he should be saying that he'd made a mistake and would find someone else.

"Do this, and you'll finally put to rest any lingering doubts anyone may have harboured since you were brought on board, doubts that your upcoming desk leave may have reinforced. After this case, they wouldn't have a leg to stand on. But if you turn it down . . ."

Was the bastard threatening her? She didn't have anything to prove to anyone! If they'd successfully completed as many operations as she had, exposed as many fraudsters and thieves, and had so many identities, they'd need a break, too.

"Director Hudson is a hands-on man. He keeps his eye on his agents."

Her hands balled into fists. She wouldn't win this battle; she'd lost it the moment Keller had phoned her. "Give me access to the file," she said through clenched teeth, then whirled and stormed from the office.

Chapter Two

J ILLIAN PUSHED OPEN the door to Room 23A at the financial district's community centre—or maybe guilt centre would be more appropriate. Donating to its upkeep allowed those with manicured nails, designer handbags, and tailored suits to stride by outstretched hands with a clear conscience. As soon as Jillian entered the large hall, the music coming from the beat-up piano in the corner reached her ears. She cursed when the words to the familiar hymn ran through her mind, and knew with a terrible certainty that Donaldson was right. She'd effortlessly slip back into the role of spiritual seeker, and hate every minute of it.

Most of the chairs were already filled with people waiting for the service to start. Some munched on lunch, a few read newspapers, and others listened to the pianist; several were on their feet, swaying to the music with their hands raised. Jillian's jaw tightened. She sat next to one of the saner attendees, whose head was bent over her smart phone. The woman didn't even glance at her. So much for community. Hypocrites! Everyone would recite the words, nod their heads at whatever Preston said, praise the Lord, and then go back into the world and behave exactly as they pleased. Except they'd feel superior to everyone else, because they'd put in their half-hour and received absolution.

As Jillian ate the lunch she'd picked up at a fast food joint, she gave the room another once-over. Sitting in her business suit with a sandwich in hand, she fit right in with the crowd. A woman with a name tag stuck to her blouse headed her way. Great. The dreaded greeter. *I'm on.* Jillian set her half-eaten sandwich on the wrapper on her lap and moved it onto the empty chair to her right, then stood and pasted a smile on her face.

The greeter—Joanna, according to the name tag pinned to her chest—responded with one of those wide, vacuous grins everyone in church wore, and extended her hand. "Welcome to our little oasis," she breathed. "Your first time here? I'm Joanna Nicholson. I work at the bank on the corner."

Jillian shook Joanna's hand. "Jillian Carter. I'm a freelance accountant, on contract right now." If Joanna asked where, Jillian would hand her a business card. The phone number would lead to an answering service; the address to one of the agency's office fronts. "I saw one of Reverend Preston's signs on a post and thought I'd come get away from the hustle and bustle."

Joanna's head bobbed. "Even half an hour makes all the difference. People don't take the time to listen, to decompress. You'll have more energy this afternoon than you usually do, I guarantee it."

Jillian doubted that. "Have you been coming here long?"

"A couple of months. Reverend Preston—" She tutted and shook her head. "He doesn't like to be called reverend. He has a very informal approach to spirituality. He's a Christian, but we welcome everyone here. He uses inclusive language. You'll see."

Jillian resisted the urge to ask about the fundraising campaign. She was supposed to be new, and hadn't received the flyer she'd read in Preston's file. Rushing things because she wanted to be anywhere but here would only blow it.

"Anyway, I'll let you get back to your lunch. The service will start in a minute or two."

"Nice meeting you," Jillian murmured. She sat down, and had almost finished her sandwich when the pianist stopped playing and looked expectantly at a door off one side of the room, which Jillian suspected led to a kitchen. Everyone shifted their attention to the door—except for Jillian's neighbour, who was still focused on her phone. Maybe the woman had come so she could work through lunch hour without anyone bothering her.

The door swung open. Preston strode into the hall, nodding and smiling at those he recognized. Due to his recent file photo, Jillian could have picked him out of a crowd. "Welcome, everyone," Preston boomed. "Let's put aside our newspapers, phones, netbooks, and e-readers."

Jillian's neighbour switched off her phone and shoved it into her purse. Who said miracles didn't happen? The inevitable coughs filled the air as Preston closed his eyes and clasped his hands in front of him. Oh, please. Jillian lowered her head. At this type of gathering, she could duck her head any time she needed to hide her face, without worrying about what anyone would think. She looked up when Preston cleared his throat.

He nodded to the pianist. The words to a modern song with spiritual undertones appeared on the screen near the piano. Hearing everyone sing gave Jillian chills; suddenly she was a little girl, clutching Mom's hand and mouthing words she didn't understand, her eyes on Dad sitting proudly—she forced her mind back to the present, and wanted to sneer at the room filled with sheep. The Bible had that right. Sheep, all of them, with Preston their shepherd, leading them not to greener pastures, but to the slaughter.

The service that followed strove to be inclusive by bending over backward to be spiritual, not religious: inspirational songs rather than hymns, a motivational talk that would have made Tony Robbins proud, and moments of meditation instead of prayer. All in all, a rather typical church service dressed up as something else. Apparently "inclusive" meant bilking donors of *all* religions of their hard-earned money.

Jillian didn't give a crap about the corporations that might line Preston's pockets with five-figure donations from petty cash. She'd come for the regular working Joe and Jane who hadn't figured out that Preston was a con artist. That went for all religious institutions and their collection plates, but she couldn't do anything about them, and she'd held her nose and dropped a ten-dollar bill into the bowl passed along her row. The woman next to her had donated twenty dollars. Guilt money.

Having fulfilled whatever need or obligation had brought them here, most of those in the hall grabbed their purses and briefcases and hurried back into the real world. Jillian took her time, sauntering over to a wastebasket to dispose of her lunch garbage, then standing hunched over her phone as she surreptitiously watched Preston chat with a couple of keeners. When the group finally broke up and Preston walked toward Joanna, who was shaking everyone's hand as they filed from the hall, Jillian made her move. She stepped into Preston's path. "Sorry," she murmured when he stopped short.

"That's all ri—" He looked at her, and froze.

Was she being too obvious? "I should watch where I'm going. Too focused on my phone," she said, holding it up.

His face relaxed; he chuckled. "Any illusions I had that everyone is contemplating my stirring words as they return to work just went down the drain. I'm Jim Preston, but I guess you already know that." He stuck out his hand.

She shook it. "Jillian Carter," she said, noting that he hadn't used his title to lord authority over her.

"Jillian Carter," he repeated slowly, his eyes boring into her. Uncomfortable, she shifted her weight. "I haven't seen you here before," he finally said.

"No, this is my first time. I enjoyed the service. I'm looking forward to Wednesday."

"I'm glad we'll see you again. We're—"

A man appeared at his elbow. "Reverend Preston, Mr. Edwards would like a word about the fundraiser next week."

Preston nodded. "Sorry," he said to Jillian. "I've put off Mr. Edwards for too long."

"Nice meeting you," Jillian said, not surprised at Preston's eagerness to speak with Edwards, nor upset by the interruption. She'd accomplished what she came to do: establish contact.

"And you," Preston returned. "Let's continue our conversation on Wednesday." He smiled, then walked away.

She'd gladly speak to him again. Next time, Jillian would be one of the keeners; she'd corner Preston after the service and ask about a point he'd raised in his talk. In a couple of weeks, she'd volunteer to help with the fundraising. Yep, she'd become one of Preston's biggest fans and most ardent supporters.

Joanna beamed at her. "So what did you think?"

"I can see why people are talking about it."

"We have to put out more chairs every week. That's why we're hoping to buy a building we can call our own. But first we're raising funds for a soup kitchen we'll run out of this centre." She twisted to pick up a flyer from the table next to her and handed it to Jillian. "We're holding our first auction next week. I'm sure we'll have something you want. Every little bit helps."

Jillian thanked her for the flyer she'd already read and left. Out on the sidewalk, she slipped on her sunglasses and headed for her fake office. Nobody would follow her—she wasn't working that type of assignment—but she wasn't a sloppy agent. As she strolled, she contemplated Preston's service, but not in a way he'd appreciate. So far, so good. Contact made, and Preston's minion had already broached the fundraising subject. Jillian would expect a soft sell to move to a hard sell, especially when Preston and those in on his game noticed how enthusiastic she was about helping him to do his good work. They'd rub their hands together in glee at the thought of emptying her bank account, and she'd let them do it, while she gathered the evidence that proved they were planning to skip town with all those lovely donations.

JILLIAN WAVED GOOD-BYE to Joanna and left the community centre. Once again, her daily report to Donaldson would be boring. As much as she hated to admit it, Jim Preston appeared to be on the up and up. Over the past six weeks, Jim, Joanna, and the handful of people in Jim's inner circle had welcomed and embraced her. When he'd found out about her super accounting and financial skills, Jim had suggested that she give Mike, his "finance guy," a hand, and Mike had given her access to the financial records for Jim's organization. They were squeaky clean. Money went exactly where Mike said it went. Her investigation into Jim's background hadn't turned up anything, either. Not a whiff of a scandal. No bilked seniors left in his wake, no collapsed pyramid schemes. Nothing had set off alarm bells. What had brought him to Donaldson's attention? Preston's file was vague on that point, and when she'd asked Donaldson, he'd brushed the question aside.

Curiously, Donaldson wasn't growing impatient. Jillian hadn't suggested they were wasting their time—yet. But how long would Donaldson keep her on a wild goose chase? Surely Keller must be getting antsy by now, wondering when he'd get his agent back, and

Jillian was growing tired of working two- or three-hour days. She wasn't one for twiddling her thumbs, and all the free time drove home how empty her life had become. No friends, no hobbies, and no point in investing in either. After this case, she'd do her stint on desk duty, go back into the field, and become best friends with her new co-workers, taking on their interests and pastimes while she snooped into their affairs behind their backs. At least she'd spent more than a couple of weeks sleeping in her own apartment, rather than in a house in another city with furnishings and décor she hadn't chosen. It had been years . . .

She stopped at the corner and waited for the light to change.

"Excuse me. Do you have the time?"

Jillian turned to her right. She gripped her satchel's handle; her instincts screeched at her to get away! She had to stop herself from sprinting across the street against the red light. Why? The business-man blinking at her looked perfectly benign. She shook herself and checked her watch. "Almost one."

"Thank you."

The light changed. Jillian crossed the road and continued walking, aware that the man had crossed with her and still strolled at her side. "You go to the lunch hour services at the community centre, don't you?" he said.

"Yes," she said warily. She couldn't recall seeing him there, but some people showed up to see what the fuss was about and never came again.

"What do you think of Reverend Preston?"

She shrugged. "He's okay. What do you think of him?" she asked, sure that he must have attended a service and she hadn't noticed him.

He ignored her question. "Do you work with him, or just pop in to listen to him speak?"

The hairs on the back of her neck stood up. The compulsion to run gripped her. She glanced over her shoulder and quickly hailed the cab heading in their direction. "Thank god, I thought I'd never see one. Late for a meeting," she said as the cab pulled up to the curb. She gave the man a strained smile as she opened the cab's back door. "Have a nice day." Without waiting for a reply, she climbed into the back seat and pulled the door shut.

"Where to?" the cabby said.

"What?" The blood pounding in Jillian's ears made it difficult to hear herself think, let alone the cab driver. She swallowed and clung to the satchel on her lap.

"Where do you want to go?"

"Oh, right." She gave him the address for her apartment, suddenly wanting to go home, lock the door, and climb under a blanket. She usually didn't panic like this.

As the cab pulled out and merged into traffic, she glimpsed the man continuing on his way, and felt silly. He'd merely asked her the time and then tried to strike up a conversation with her. Maybe he'd found her attractive, or was being polite. Or maybe he wanted to attend one of the services, but needed to know that he'd find a familiar face and have someone to sit with. She might have wanted to get away from him because he subconsciously reminded her of one of Dad's associates.

No, she'd trust her instincts; they'd never failed her. His questions had struck her as strange. Why had he asked if she worked with Jim? If he liked her, why hadn't he asked for her name and number, or where she worked, or talked about the weather? Why had she recoiled the moment she'd laid eyes on him?

Forget about cowering in her bedroom. Before she called Donaldson, she'd go over Jim's records with a fine tooth comb to make sure she hadn't missed anything. Her gut told her that the strange man's interest in her association with Jim hadn't been innocent, but she'd need more than that to satisfy Donaldson.

Chapter Three

RUMINATING OVER THE day's events, Jillian strolled home from the grocery store, a bag in each hand. Her review of Jim's records had turned up nothing. Next time she spoke to Donaldson, she'd recommend winding down her involvement with Jim's group. Surprisingly, she felt that abruptly pulling out and leaving Jim in the lurch wouldn't be right. They were a good group of people—misguided, but sincere. After the fundraising concert next week, she'd catch Jim alone and tell him that his message wasn't clicking with her, that she hadn't minded helping out, but didn't want to be a hypocrite. Wow, this was the first time her exit story would be one hundred percent true.

Would she rather that Jim focus his energies on helping and inspiring people without the religious mumbo-jumbo undertones? Absolutely. But when it came to the harm religion caused, his organization was a flea amongst giants, and nobody left his meetings brainwashed and burdened with guilt. Jillian wouldn't lose any sleep over people choosing to spend their lunch hour in a room at the community centre, listening to Jim speak about taking the time to smell the roses. Better yet, Jim didn't pretend to be perfect, didn't put himself on a pedestal, wasn't power hungry, and didn't urge his followers to go out and convert everybody. He certainly didn't covet wealth. If all groups were like his, she wouldn't wish that religion be wiped off the face of the earth. Walking past a church wouldn't set her teeth on edge. She wouldn't want to shake sense into anyone who believed in God.

In her apartment building's lobby, she waited impatiently for the elevator, wondering why one of them appeared to be stuck on her floor. Finally an elevator door dinged open, the car going up. A minute later, she unlocked her apartment door. The phone was ringing—the land line, not the one in her front pocket. She kicked the door shut and dropped the grocery bags to the floor, then went to the phone in the living room.

"Hello," she said as she flicked on a lamp.

"Jillian?"

"Yes."

"It's Jim Preston."

"Hi, Jim," she said, hoping she sounded casual. She never spoke to Jim on the phone; she always called Mike when she had a question. Then her blood ran cold. How the hell could Jim have her land line number? It was listed under her real name. "What can I do for you?" she asked, her mind racing.

"Donaldson is using you."

She felt as if Jim had slapped her. "Who?"

Jim sighed. "I know who you are and what you're doing, so let's cut the bull, okay? We need to talk."

Her hand tightened around the receiver. How could she salvage this disaster? Her cover was blown. At this point, all she could do was gather information. Even if she'd somehow given herself away, how had Jim discovered her true identity? Did they have a snitch in Donaldson's department? "Okay, I'll bite. Why do you think Donaldson is using me?"

"Not on the phone. I'm in the neighbourhood. I'll be there in five minutes."

Jesus, he knew where she lived, too. "Don't come here." He must think she was crazy. No way would she allow him to get her alone in her apartment. "If you have something to say, say it."

"It would be better if I could talk to you in person. If you don't want me in your apartment, how about meeting me somewhere?"

Like a back alley? "Do you think the phone is tapped? Listen, we have nothing to talk about. Since you know who I really am, we won't be seeing each other again. Good-bye," she said, not intending to hang up.

"Jillian!"

Good.

"Are you still there?"

"Yes." She could hear him breathing.

"You're not who you say you are. Well, neither am I. Donaldson told you that I'm a con man, right? You're working with Mike because you're hoping to uncover financial wrong-doing."

Jillian hesitated, then said, "Yes." There was no point denying what he already knew, and she wanted to keep him talking, to find out who the hell was leaking information. How could Jim know what angle she was investigating? Wait, could he have access to her case history? Considering she normally worked financial cases, it wouldn't be difficult to put two and two together, especially if he was committing fraud.

"It's all a pretense, Jillian. He gave you a bogus case so he could use you to find out why I'm in town."

"Why would he do that?"

"Because he works for people who are interested in me and an organization I belong to. He chose you because he wanted someone vulnerable, so he could discredit them if they figured out that he's dirty. He'd tell you to come in and then turn on you, painting you as disturbed, unreliable, unable to do your job. He'd use your pysch eval to have you locked up—permanently."

Her mortification deepened. What didn't Jim know? "You're saying Donaldson is dirty, the operation I'm on is a sham, and he chose me so that if I figured that all out myself, he could easily shut me up."

"Exactly. Have you wondered why he asked for you? Don't you think it's strange that out of all the agents he could have used, he wanted you?"

Anxiety snaked through her. She'd had similar thoughts when Donaldson was telling her about the case. "No, I don't think it's strange."

"What about your father, your history?"

Jim's knowledge of her background didn't alarm her. Her father's pathetic death and the reasons behind it had dominated the front pages of the newspapers for days. But that didn't mean she wanted to discuss it. "What are you expecting me to do? Go in and accuse Donaldson of making up cases? What proof do you have?"

"I don't care about Donaldson. I care about you. You're the reason I'm in town. The organization I belong to . . . you're meant to join us."

She blew out an exasperated sigh. "I'll need more information than that."

"Let me come over—"

"No."

"It's going to sound far-fetched."

"That's your problem, not mine." She eyed the sofa but remained standing, too keyed up to sit. "What organization are you talking about?"

Silence, then, "I belong to a group that investigates and deals with situations that threaten the balance between Good and Evil in our world. We root out corruption, including that within religious organizations."

Jillian snorted. "You must be awfully busy, and you're not doing a very good job."

"Satan's agents, known as Beguilers, work against us," Jim said.

Okay, the conversation had just entered the loony zone, but she had to keep him talking. "So you fight against these, uh, satanic agents," Jillian said, hoping she sounded sincere and interested. "I'm still not clear on what any of this has to do with me and Donaldson."

"Satan isn't the only one with agents," Jim said calmly. "God has agents, too. I'm one of them."

She gaped. Thank god they weren't having this conversation in person.

"And so are you," Jim added.

"What?" Her amusement turned to anger. "Enough, already! What does this have to do with Donaldson?"

"He works with the Beguilers. If he finds out I'm here for you, he'll put his fallback plan into action and have you committed, so they can try to turn you."

If anybody needed committing, it wasn't her.

"It's time for you to join us," Jim said.

She stifled a laugh with her hand. He sounded so lucid at the community centre. Had he forgotten to take his medication, or something? "Let me see if I have this right. I'm some God agent, and you're here to recruit me into your merry band." She winced at her levity. *Don't lose him.*

"I was told to come and get you, yes."

By God, no doubt. If someone suddenly cut in on their conversation and informed her that this was an elaborate joke, she wouldn't be surprised.

"The man who spoke to you earlier today, after you left the centre. You sensed danger. You had to get away from him."

"What man?" Jillian said, shocked.

"The man I saw talking to you on the corner. I saw him, Jillian."

Jillian shrugged, despite her growing uneasiness. "He asked me the time, then started to chat. It's not the first time a man's struck up a conversation with me on a sidewalk."

"He set off alarm bells because he was a Beguiler. They're growing impatient. Donaldson hasn't figured out why I'm hanging around town, so they're doubling their efforts. If they find out you're the one I'm interested in . . . please, listen to me. You're in danger. Let me come over. I can protect you, get you to safety."

"How did you find out about me and my investigation?" Normally she wouldn't be so blunt, but these weren't normal circumstances. Jim just might tell her.

"We work for someone who knows everything," Jim murmured.

Okay, she'd had enough of this crap. "I don't believe you, and I don't believe in God."

"You don't believe in God?" Jim said, his bewilderment coming through loud and clear.

"No. And as far as I can tell, I'm not some freaking God agent." This was pointless. Her cover was blown, and Jim was apparently off his rocker. "I'm hanging up."

"No! Let me—"

"If you're a man of God, you'll stop harassing me."

"I can prove it to you. If you'll just let me come over—"

"No, no, and no! If I see you anywhere near my apartment, I'll call the police. Stay away from me."

"Jillian—"

She hung up, then lifted the receiver to call Donaldson. But doubt held her back. It *was* strange that Donaldson had specifically wanted her. The man on the street *had* set her heart racing for no apparent reason. Jim's books were clean, and he knew about Donaldson, her psych eval, everything. So . . . Jim was some type of God agent? Right.

Jim was delusional, but not harmless. Somehow he had access to confidential records, and she hadn't discovered the source of the leak. If not for her brainwashing as a child, she wouldn't be waffling. But telling Donaldson that Jim believed she was some sort of chosen one . . . no. Donaldson needed to know the following: Jim had called to tell her that he knew her real identity and to try to convince her that Donaldson was dirty. He'd also claimed to work for some bizarre religious organization and that he acted on behalf of God, something Donaldson had probably heard a zillion times before. Forget the nonsense about her. The agency needed facts, not unicorns. She mentally rehearsed what she'd say, then dialed Donaldson.

After listening to her account of her conversation with Jim, Donaldson said, "I'm sending a team to go over your apartment. He knows where you live. He might have dropped in when you weren't there. Our guys should be there within ten minutes. You have access to a firearm?"

"It's locked away. I normally don't work the sorts of cases that require one."

"Get it, in case Preston shows up before we get there. And don't worry, we'll keep an eye on the place until we catch up with," his voice hardened, "Reverend Preston."

AT EIGHT-THIRTY ON the dot the next morning, Jillian paced in front of Donaldson's desk. She swung to face him and folded her arms. "He knew everything. You, me, what I was doing. Someone's leaking information."

Amazingly calm, Donaldson leaned back in his chair. "Let me worry about that." She opened her mouth to protest, then clamped it shut when Donaldson raised his hand. "You're out of it now. We'll handle the," his mouth turned up at the corners, "God agent."

Her fingers dug into her arms. She'd never botched an operation before. Botched? This was a freaking disaster. To maintain her fragile reputation, she'd sit meekly at a desk and shuffle papers for a while.

Donaldson chuckled. "You know, in my position, you hear a ton of weird conspiracy shit, and I don't think there's a famous person, dead or alive, who hasn't been labelled the second coming or the antichrist. You think you've heard it all, and then something comes along that's on a whole new level of crazy." He paused. "So Preston didn't say who he's looking for?"

"No, he just said he was here to recruit someone."

"I wonder why he called *you*."

"I don't know. I've asked myself the same thing. His financials are clean, so I don't understand why he'd go off the deep end like that. I was on the verge of suggesting that we terminate the operation because Preston is genuine."

Donaldson shrugged. "Maybe he thought you were getting close to uncovering his scheme and hoped to distract you, or to convince you to go in with him."

But Jim must have known there was nothing for her to find, at least not in his financial records. She'd gone over his books forward, backward, and sideways. Then again, she wasn't infallible. There was a tiny chance she'd missed something. "Even so, why come up with such an outlandish story, instead of warning me away, or insisting that we were unfairly investigating him, or making me an offer he figured I couldn't refuse?" Especially since he knew about her father. Bringing God into it was the worst approach Jim could have taken.

"Have you considered that he believes what he told you? Preston *is* a religious man—supposedly."

Jillian snickered. "How could any rational person—"

"Sit in my chair for a week and the crap that rational people believe won't surprise you anymore. Frighten you? Yes. Make you laugh? Sometimes. Surprise you? No. Preston probably believes he's under the protection of," Donaldson looked at the ceiling and raised his arms, "the Lord."

Jillian couldn't help but laugh. "If he does believe he's untouchable, he might show up at the community centre for the lunch service tomorrow. I can go—"

Donaldson vigorously shook his head and jabbed his finger on his desk. "Leave Preston to us. I know it stings when your cover is blown, but in a roundabout way, you did your job. You rattled him. You made him show his hand. If Preston was legitimate, he'd know diddly-squat about us. We won't rest until we find out how he's getting his information. He's no longer your problem."

Donaldson was right. As much as she'd relish it, marching into the community centre and publicly calling Jim a fraud wouldn't accomplish anything. Jim's "flock" would think *she* was the lunatic. She dropped her arms to her sides and sighed. "I'll go see Keller."

"Good idea." Donaldson rolled back his chair and stood. "Don't worry, we'll get him, and we'll plug the leak." He held out his hand. "Thank you for your service, Agent Campbell. I just might call on you again."

She hoped not, but she nodded as she shook his hand and made a point of meeting Donaldson's eyes. No racing heart, no shivers running up her spine. But then, he wasn't a—what had Jim called them? A Beguiler. No, he just worked for them. Jillian quickly left Donaldson's office before the giggle bubbling up inside her escaped.

She'd expected Keller to show her to her temporary desk, but he had other ideas. "Go home," he said. "Both Donaldson and I think a short break will do you good. I'll see you on Monday."

She drew breath to insist that she didn't need time off, then changed her mind. Ever since she'd called home after completing her last operation for Keller, Mom had nagged her to visit. Why not get the dreaded family time over with now, when Jillian wouldn't mind staying somewhere other than her apartment for a few days? As soon as she left Keller's office, she pulled out her phone.

Chapter Four

Jillian dragged her eyes away from the TV and checked the wall clock. Only 2:45. How time crawled when you weren't having fun!

"Oh, he's about to reveal the paternity test results." Mom straightened in her chair. "All hell's going to break loose."

Jillian watched, unmoved by all the tears and shouting. But as the show guests continued to scream at each other, anger simmered within her, threatening to boil over. Who in their right mind went on TV to bare their sordid little lives and problems? When Dad's name had been all over the papers and his downfall was the lead story on every newscast, she'd wanted to crawl into a hole and die. She recalled her mother's bewilderment and grief, the hushed voices, her own dawning understanding that Dad was not only gone, but reviled, and that she and her mother were "innocent victims," according to a local pastor. That hadn't stopped the kids at school from taunting her. *"Your father was a liar! If your dad hadn't killed himself, we would have done it for him. Guess your dad didn't love you, huh? He shot himself because he couldn't stand to be with you."*

She shot up from the sofa.

"Where are you going, honey?" Mom asked, her eyes still on the TV. "The show's not over."

"I need to do something, Mom. I'm tired of watching TV."

"Wait until this is over and then we'll go shopping. I need to get a few things for dinner."

"No, I'll go. I feel like some time alone."

Mom didn't argue. "Rolls, carrots, butter, and potatoes."

Jillian silently repeated the list to herself a couple of times.

"Oh, and pick up a bottle of wine, too."

"Sure."

Outside on the porch, Danny lifted his head from his book and pushed his reading glasses up his nose. "Escaping for a bit?"

She nodded. "What are you reading?" she asked, even though she could guess the answer. Danny's impressive coin and stamp collections occupied an entire room in the house. He spent hours poring over catalogues while Mom sat glued to the TV. Jillian wouldn't knock it; it worked for them. Sure enough, he showed her the cover of a coin catalogue.

"Anything you want me to pick up from the mall?" She could go to the grocery store two blocks away, but she'd rather drive to the mall and stroll mindlessly through it for an hour or two.

Danny shook his head. "I'll see you later." He lifted a brow. "I think it's cards tonight."

Jillian smiled and patted his shoulder. "Sounds like fun." She expected his nose to be back in his catalogue by the time she pulled out of the driveway and cruised past the house, but she glanced his way and waved anyway, and smiled again when he waved back.

Danny's appearance in their lives had signalled a turning point, though she hadn't appreciated him until she was older. At fifteen, she hadn't wanted a stepfather and had behaved like the typical spoiled brat, rebuffing him whenever he tried to talk to her, accusing Mom of caring more about him than her, and throwing tantrums every time Mom had insisted they all go out to dinner, or a movie, or camping for a weekend. Fortunately her antics hadn't put Danny off, and Mom had married him, one of her more intelligent decisions. Over time, Danny's persistence and quiet but firm support had won Jillian over.

Her mouth tightened. How she'd treated Danny was one of her biggest regrets. Telling herself that she'd had every reason to reject a father figure never made her feel any better. He hadn't deserved her crap. She wanted to tell him she was sorry, but she didn't want to upset their comfortable relationship. Plus, talking about feelings, about regrets, wasn't done in her family. If she and Mom had supported each other, shared their fear, anger, and disbelief, instead of retreating into their own private hells, maybe their relationship wouldn't be so

"It could be less serious than we think. Right now, all they're saying is that they're looking for a person of interest. They haven't released your information to the media."

"They told my mother I killed somebody," Jillian snapped.

Donaldson tutted. "Scare tactics. They do want to find you. I'll call the lead detective on the case, let him know that you're on your way here. We're working on finding out what evidence they have that incriminates you. By the time you get here, they might not be interested in you anymore. At the very least, you'll have a damn good lawyer running interference."

Donaldson's calm voice and reassuring words helped Jillian regain some perspective. She was innocent. The agency would stand behind her. It was all a terrible mistake. "I'm on my way."

As she walked through the parking lot, she half expected to hear, "Police! Freeze!" ring out, but nobody gave her a second glance. Her phone rang as she buckled her seatbelt. *Unknown number.* Normally she'd let it go through to voice mail, but on a day like today . . . "Hello."

"Don't go to Donaldson," a male voice said.

"Excuse me?"

"If you're lucky, he'll kill you. If you're not so lucky, you'll spend the rest of your life in solitary confinement."

"Who is this?"

"A friend of Jim's."

"Let me guess. You're a God agent?" Jillian shook her head. "How did you get this number?" She'd already removed the forwarding of "Jillian Carter's" number, so this person had her agency number.

"There's no time for this. Go to Donaldson, and you'll walk right into a trap. Come to us instead. We're your only hope now."

She snorted. "And I'm supposed to take your word for it? Run away and make myself look guiltier than sin? And then what? You'll protect me? You'll work some voodoo and get the police to drop the charges? Please."

"Jillian, I know you're skeptical," he said, sounding annoyed, "but I'm trying to help you."

"No, you're trying to convince me to turn away from the people who have the best shot at helping me."

"Donaldson is lying to you."

"Why would he lie to me? I didn't do it! It's a mistake."

"The police have evidence up the wazoo that points to you."

She thumped the steering wheel with her free hand. "That's not possible," she shouted. *Calm down. Don't let this fool get to you.* She took a deep breath. "I don't know who you are, or what you're really up to when it comes to me." Especially since she worked white-collar crime. She could understand a criminal organization wanting to have an agent in narcotics or the like in its back pocket. What would they want with her? Money laundering? Surely they could come up with something better than the cockamamie story they'd fed her so far. She didn't know whether to dismiss them as crackpots, or have the appropriate section open an investigation into what amounted to harassment. Could this have anything to do with Dad? Was someone getting off on harassing his daughter—twenty-five years later? To what end? It wouldn't make sense.

"We're only trying to help you. The first step is to get rid of your car. We'll pick you up. Drive to the corner of—"

"I don't want your help. Don't contact me again." She hung up, started the car, and drove out of the parking lot. When her phone rang again, she turned it off. She went to flick on the radio, then jerked her hand back, not wanting to hear the reports about Jim and Joanna. She didn't need that right now; it would only freak her out, especially since doubts were stirring. How had the caller gotten her number? How did he know she was going to Donaldson, and what evidence the police had? What if the agency's intervention with the police didn't get her off the hook? What if Donaldson was setting her up? Maybe she should have allowed her mystery caller to finish his instructions, just in case.

God, listen to me! She was letting the caller play with her mind. She was innocent. The police couldn't have evidence that didn't exist. Some idiot detective had put two and two together and gotten five. As Donaldson had said, she was a person of interest, nothing more. After clearing up this mess, she *would* request an investigation into the mystery call. Enough was enough.

She felt the tension drain from her when she drove into the underground parking garage at work. In an hour or two, she'd laugh about this and shake her head at how gullible some people were.

When she called Mom to apologize for not showing up at the house, she'd have to curtail her irritation over Mom believing that she could kill someone. Honestly! Though, to be fair, Mom had called to warn her; she hadn't pointed the cops to the mall, and having police bang on the door and refer to her daughter as a murder suspect must have frightened her.

With a sigh, Jillian got out of her car and walked toward the elevator.

"Police! Down on your knees! Down on your knees!"

Her heart leaped into her mouth. She froze. Cops were everywhere. Uniformed officers slowly approached her, their guns drawn.

"Down on your knees, Campbell! Now!" The loud voices echoed around the garage.

"I'm here to see someone who'll sort this out," she said as she slowly knelt.

"Hands behind your head!"

She complied. Police swarmed her. Her hands were yanked from her head and held behind her back. Cold metal encircled her wrists. "This is a mistake!" she shouted as they roughly hauled her to her feet. "I came here to clear this up. I work for the government. My superior is upstairs, waiting for me. I'll give you a number to call."

A burly cop grabbed her left arm and steered her toward a waiting unmarked car. Were they all deaf? A hand pushed down on her head and forced her into the car's backseat. The door slammed. Jillian's throat tightened. Two policemen climbed into the front seats. "This is all a mistake. I didn't do it," she croaked as the car pulled away.

The two men in front glanced at each other and shook their heads.

JILLIAN HOPPED OFF the police van and grimaced when she landed hard. She lumbered after the corrections officer, hindered by her shackled ankles. Shouts filled the air.

"Why'd you do it, Jillian?"

"Marcy Abrams from News World Five. Do you have anything to say?"

"Murderer!"

She glanced in the direction of the ruckus, then quickly faced forward. Images of her shuffling into the courthouse would fill TV screens; everyone would see a cold-blooded double murderer restrained like an animal. Were Mom and Danny in the courtroom?

The officer held open the courthouse's side door; another officer entered first, then turned to grasp her arm and pull her through the doorway. The few people they passed in the corridor didn't gawk, but their pace slowed and their eyes flicked to Jillian's face. Even though she defiantly stared at them, she felt guilty, and probably looked it, too. She'd endured enough sneers, dirty looks, and smirks to know that shouting, "I'm innocent!" would hurt, not help.

Her heart sank when one of the officers ushered her into the room where her lawyer waited. Well, she'd kidded herself, hoping Donaldson would come through and replace the lawyer she'd found in the yellow pages with someone who had more than five minutes' experience. Catherine Trotter sat fidgeting at a square table. This time, she'd better have come with more than bleated apologies about not knowing what evidence the cops had gathered. When Jillian was free, the first thing she'd do was find another law firm, one that would send out a senior partner for a double murder case—not that she anticipated ever needing one for that reason again.

The corrections officer pulled out a chair and pushed her into it. "I'll be right outside the door," he growled to Trotter.

Jillian lifted her hands. "Can I have these off?"

"While you're in here, alone with her?" He snorted. "Not bloody likely."

She almost retorted, "Why, do you think I'll kill her?" but thought better of it. Trotter would probably bolt from the room, screaming. She rested her hands on her lap. The door closed.

Trotter laid her satchel on the table, opened it, and pulled out a file. "Read this over," she said, removing a sheet of paper from the file and sliding it across the table.

Jillian stiffened when she read the first paragraph on the page. "Why are you arranging a plea bargain? I'm not guilty."

Trotter blinked at her. "If you won't be honest with me, I can't help you."

"I didn't do it."

"Nobody can hear us. Anything you tell me—"

"I didn't do it!" She glared at Trotter. "I'm innocent."

Trotter lifted a brow. She pulled a photograph from the file and tossed it onto the table. "Recognize that?"

Jillian frowned. "It could be my gun."

"It is your gun. It's also the murder weapon."

"What?"

Another sheet landed on the table. "Witness statements, placing you at the location where the bodies were found."

She gaped. Her mind went blank.

"Phone records show that you called Jim Preston shortly before he and his associate were last seen. In fact, yours was the last call on his phone."

"I've never called Jim Preston," Jillian said, managing to find her voice. "He called me once. That's the only time we ever spoke on the phone."

"Not according to Preston's records."

"Did the phone call come from my cell, or the land line in my apartment?"

Trotter consulted another paper from the infernal file. "The land line."

"It doesn't matter, anyway. I didn't call him, and I never saw him outside the community centre. Ever."

Trotter's eyes met Jillian's. "Come on, Ms. Campbell, nobody is going to believe that you and Preston weren't close."

"Why not?"

Trotter cleared her throat. "Preston's semen was found on your bed, along with several of his pubic hairs."

"What?" she shrieked. "No! We weren't lovers. We weren't even friends." And since she was into women, he definitely hadn't been her type. But she'd spent her life firmly in the closet. Coming out to Trotter wouldn't help; she'd come across as willing to say anything to save her ass. *If you're not so lucky, you'll spend the rest of your life in solitary confinement.* "Can't you see I'm being set up? Tons of people have traipsed through my apartment recently. Anyone could have taken my gun, planted the semen, used my phone . . . if I did it and wanted to get away, why would I go to my mother's?"

"So you're accusing government agents of planting evidence in your apartment?" Trotter gave her a dubious look. "Your agency is doing all it can to help you. In fact, it was instrumental in putting the plea bargain together."

"At the very least, you'll have a damn good lawyer running interference." Bastard.

"And since you're still technically innocent, it will protect you. It's feeding the media your usual cover story . . . for now." Trotter moistened her lips and leaned forward. "What would have happened if your superiors found out that you were carrying on with the man you were investigating? Did you find dirt on Preston, and he threatened to tell your superiors about your relationship if you blew the whistle on him? That's why you killed him, isn't it? Because you were afraid he'd take you down with him. Or was he blackmailing you?"

Jillian would have laughed, if her wrists and ankles weren't shackled and the story sounded less plausible. "Why did I kill Joanna?"

"You tell me. Was she in the wrong place at the wrong time?"

Jesus. "When I skipped town, why didn't I take the gun with me?"

Trotter's brow furrowed. "You did. The police found it in your car, with your fingerprints all over it. Nobody else's."

Her blood ran cold.

"Enough with the lies. Shall we start again?" Trotter reached across the table and tapped the sheet with the plea bargain details. "Unless you can convince me that you shot them in self-defence, this is the best you're going to get. You'll be a senior citizen when you next taste freedom." Her mouth twisted. "But your two victims will never see freedom again, so some still wouldn't call it justice."

No, they should call it an injustice! Donaldson—or someone else—had done his job well. No jury on earth would acquit her, but she wouldn't surrender her innocence for a shorter sentence. Accepting the plea bargain would be the same as admitting guilt. She'd rather rot in jail. "Aren't you supposed to be on my side? Listen, I didn't do it. I'm not signing this."

"At least read it."

"I'm not signing it," Jillian said flatly.

Trotter's face tightened. "So you want to enter a plea of not guilty. I'm not a miracle worker. I'll do my best, but with this evidence . . . maybe we can work the mental health angle. I read your file. Your father was a pastor, Preston was a pastor. You were lovers, but he was over twenty years older than you. Was it really about your father? Did you see him when you pulled the trigger?"

Jillian felt her face flush. "You are one sick bitch!" she spat, then regretted her outburst when Trotter recoiled. Deep breath. "I'm not making any deals. I'm not guilty. That's what you'll say when—"

Someone rapped at the door and swung it open. "Excuse me, Ms. Trotter." A man in a three piece business suit, briefcase in hand, stepped in and stopped next to Jillian. "I'm Peter Dryden. I've been engaged to take over Ms. Campbell's case." He handed a business card to Trotter, who was already rising. She barely glanced at it before sliding it into her satchel's side pocket. "A little bird told me there's a plea bargain in the works," Dryden said.

Trotter nodded. "I'm sure they'll offer you the same deal, if you ask. Good luck getting her to take it, though." She returned all the papers to her satchel and rounded the table. "She's all yours." The door closed behind her.

Still standing next to Jillian, Dryden grunted. She twisted to look up at him. Was she wrong about Donaldson, or had Mom and Danny managed to scrape together the money for Dryden? "Who hired you?"

"We don't have time to discuss that now. We're due in court."

"I'm not guilty. I'm not taking any deal."

He nodded. "I understand."

A lump formed in her throat. "You won't advise me to take a deal?"

"No. I wasn't hired to make a deal."

To her horror, tears sprang to her eyes.

He peered down at her and roughly patted her shoulder. "Don't worry. We'll do everything we can to introduce doubt."

Introduce doubt, not prove her innocence. She'd take it.

Dryden sat in the chair Trotter had vacated and snapped open his briefcase. "I have a few questions before we go in." He pulled out a legal pad and poised a pen over it. "What time did you leave for your mother's on Thursday?"

She lifted her cuffed hands and scratched her shoulder. "Around six-thirty, right after dinner."

He scribbled on the pad. "What time did you leave work?"

"Arou—awou—" Her mouth wouldn't obey her brain. Her arms felt heavy. The room spun.

"Ms. Campbell?" His words sounded distorted and loud. "Ms. Campbell?"

She slid off the chair.

"Ms. Campbell!"

Cool tile met her cheek. She blinked at the table leg. Her breathing sounded unnaturally loud. She couldn't move.

A shout rang out: "We need a doctor!"

Darkness.

Chapter Five

J ILLIAN STUMBLED AND *fell, bruising her knees on the concrete. "I'm innocent!"*

"That's what they all say." The prison guard swung the windowless metal door shut.

No! She threw herself against the door, beat it with her fists. "You can't leave me here!" But they had. Two life terms. No chance of parole. Solitary confinement. Just her and these four walls—forever.

The hairs on the back of her neck stood up. Someone was behind her. She turned around . . .

Her eyes flew open; her mind cleared. It was a dream, just a dream. Then the last moments before she'd lost consciousness rushed back.

"Ms. Campbell?"

"We need a doctor!"

But she wasn't in a hospital bed, and she faced a wall with flowered wallpaper. A surge of hope that it had *all* been a dream, that she lay in Mom's guest room after waking up from a sordid nightmare, quickly died. Dreams didn't feel that real, and the room at Mom's wasn't wallpapered. Neither were cells.

She listened. Muffled voices. A ticking clock. No traffic. Confident that nobody else was in the room, she rolled over, then covered her eyes when the sun beaming through the picture window on the opposite wall hit her in the face. Squinting, she sat up and threw the thin blanket aside. She still had on the clothes she'd worn to the courthouse, but someone had removed her shoes. The clock on the night table read *4:45*. Assuming she'd collapsed that morning, she was missing almost eight hours.

Her legs shook when she stood. She gripped the nightstand for support until they stopped trembling, then shuffled to the window and looked down on a manicured lawn dotted with trees. Not a road in sight, or any other clue to her location. She turned away, feeling light-headed and queasy. Her stomach grumbled.

The muffled voices hadn't stopped. She went to the door, opened it a crack, and discovered that she was in a room at the end of a hallway. The now louder voices—one male, one female—were coming from a room across the hall. Jillian crept toward it and peered around the doorframe. A man and a woman sat opposite each other in armchairs, each holding a mug. A round coffee table on an area rug stood between them, and bookcases covered every inch of wall. Since the woman's chair was angled away from the door, Jillian didn't have a clear view of her face. The man looked vaguely familiar . . . Peter Dryden! The lawyer. Had he somehow managed to wrangle bail and transport her here? Wait. Why had she collapsed? Damn it! She jerked her head away from the doorway and focused on what they were saying—what she would have done in the first place, if her head didn't feel so fuzzy.

She stiffened when they broke off their conversation and the woman said, "Come in, Jillian."

Dryden must have seen her and given her away. Running for it wasn't an option. She had no idea where she was, no transportation, no money, no identification. But she had questions, and if the two people in the room wanted to harm her, they'd had plenty of opportunity when she was out cold. Time to find out what was going on. She swallowed and walked into the room, swaying as her head swam.

Dryden leaped to his feet and handed his mug to the woman as he passed her. "Careful," he murmured to Jillian, taking her arm and steering her to his armchair. Too queasy to protest, she sank into it and waited for the room to stop moving. The woman sitting across from her came into focus. Their eyes met.

"So you're the one," the woman said.

Jillian felt exposed, naked, as if the woman could see right into her, know her, understand her. Wilting under the woman's gaze, Jillian pretended she was on a case and sized her up: late fifties to early sixties, hair almost completely gray, intelligent and shrewd brown eyes, a few wrinkles around her eyes and mouth.

"I should check her over," Dryden said.

The woman shifted her attention to him, much to Jillian's relief.

"You must be hungry," he said to Jillian.

"Yes, but—"

"I know, you're not sure what you can stomach."

Food could wait. She needed information. "Where am I? What am I doing here? The last thing I remember—"

The woman held up her hand. "We'll talk after Peter's examined you and you've had something to eat." She rose. "I'll go to the kitchen and see what Penny can do for us."

"Broth, bread, crackers, rice, oatmeal . . ." Peter said, ticking each item off with his fingers. "For a drink, water, ginger ale, or ginger tea will do."

The woman nodded. "When you're done, why don't you take her to the conference room? I'll meet you there." She looked down at Jillian and extended her hand. "But before I leave, I'll properly introduce myself. I'm Roberta."

Jillian shook her hand. "Jillian," she murmured. To her surprise, Roberta smiled.

"I'm pleased to finally meet you, Jillian." She turned and left the room.

"Be back in a sec," Peter murmured. Apparently confident that Jillian was in no shape to flee, he darted from the room. When he returned, he set a black doctor's bag on the coffee table, opened it, and pulled out a stethoscope.

"You're not a lawyer," Jillian stated.

"Nope." Peter inserted the stethoscope's eartips into his ears.

"I hope you're a doctor."

Peter chuckled. "A sense of humour is a good sign. Yes, I'm a doctor."

"You drugged me."

"Sorry about that." He bent toward her. "I'm just going to listen to your heart." He unfastened the top two buttons of her blouse. She tensed when he slipped the stethoscope's bell underneath her sports bra and pressed it against her chest. Stethoscopes and blood pressure cuffs always made her nervous.

"Good," he murmured, then took her pulse, shone a light in her eyes, and asked her how she felt. "The vertigo and nausea should pass within the next hour or two." Peter tucked the stethoscope back into the bag. "Let's get you to the conference room. It's on the main floor."

When he offered her his arm, she gladly took it and sagged with relief when he led her past a winding staircase to an elevator. The moment she stepped onto the main floor, two black Labradors raced toward her, their tails wagging. "They won't hurt you," Peter said, when Jillian stepped back. He patted the Lab on the left. "This is Puck." His hand moved to the other dog. "And this is Raven."

Jillian slowly extended her hand and managed a smile when the two dogs sniffed it. As a girl, she'd loved the family dog and cat, but Dad had been the animal parent. After Molly and Inky had died, Mom had put her foot down. As an adult, Jillian often felt tempted to visit the animal shelter, but she wasn't home enough to have any pets.

Peter shooed Puck and Raven away and steered Jillian through the foyer and down a hallway. While the other parts of the house she'd seen were cozy and informal, the conference room exuded business. A black rectangular table sat on wall to wall carpet, with a sophisticated control panel set into its surface. A large flat screen hung on one wall, and wires snaked from several laptops to a network hub. At Peter's suggestion, Jillian chose a place without a laptop and sat down.

Roberta bustled in and set a tray in front of her. After handing a cup of coffee to Peter and lifting a second cup from the tray, she sat in the place with the control panel. "Eat," she urged Jillian.

"First tell me who you are, where I am, and how I got here," she said, despite wanting to devour a cracker.

Roberta's brows lifted. "My, you're a stubborn one." She sipped her coffee and set it on the table. "You're with the Deiform Fellowship, Jillian. This is home to one of the Christian cells. Jim was a Deiform, and Joanna was a supporter. He was to bring you into the Fellowship." She reached for her coffee, took a long drink. "Obviously something went wrong."

Jillian winced at the pain in Roberta's voice. "I didn't kill him, or Joanna."

"We know. If we thought you had, you'd be sitting in a prison cell, not here."

Unable to resist the food any longer, Jillian picked up the spoon. She still didn't buy this God agents crap, but Peter and Roberta were part of *something*, and she wasn't in a position to do anything but listen. "What do you want with me?"

"Let's start at the beginning." Roberta was silent for a moment. "Few are chosen to be Deiforms. When a Fledgling—an untrained Deiform—is destined to come to us, I somehow know. I have a connection with them. I feel it."

"We call her the Guide," Peter said. "Every cell has one."

Jillian spooned broth into her mouth. She already felt as if she was a guest at the funny farm.

"Peter's a healer," Roberta said.

When amusement tightened Jillian's throat, the broth almost went down the wrong way. "I'm surprised you didn't lay on hands and rid me of my queasiness," she blurted.

Peter grinned. "Oh, no, my healing powers don't come from God. They come from Harvard Medical School. Of course, in some circles, God and Harvard Medical School are one and the same thing."

Jillian smiled. She couldn't help but like him. "You said every cell has a Guide. So there are multiple groups?"

Roberta nodded. "We don't choose who comes to us. When it's time for a Fledgling to surface, the intended cell's Guide receives visions through prayer and meditation. I was given the name of a city. I saw the community centre. I saw Jim speaking. I knew he'd be your first contact. Well, not you, specifically, but the Fledgling's. So Jim set up shop in the community centre, and we waited for the Fledgling to arrive." She frowned. "It's always risky when a Deiform stays in one area for too long, especially out in the open like that. We knew it was only a matter of time before a Beguiler showed up. We were hoping to bring you in before then."

"Why didn't the Beguiler just kill Jim?" Jillian dipped a cracker into the broth. "As you said, Jim was out there."

"They wouldn't kill him before they figured out what he was up to." When Jillian drew breath, Roberta quickly added, "The fact that Jim was holding public meetings told them that we were probably looking for a Fledgling, but they couldn't be sure. Normally I'm given more information. We're directed to go to the Fledgling. In your case, I had the sense that we should wait for you to come to us, and not to push."

"How do you know it's me? Plenty of people attended Jim's services. It could be anyone."

Roberta shook her head. "No, Jillian. It's you. Deiforms can sense Fledglings. Jim knew it." Her voice dropped. "And I see the Lord in you."

Jillian reached for her ginger tea, inwardly cursing her trembling hand. She set the cup back on its saucer. "I never would have voluntarily joined your . . . fellowship. I had no idea, no inkling, that I'm a Fledgling. I still don't." How could she, when it was complete and utter bullshit?

"We weren't expecting you to show up one day and say, hey, I'm ready now." Peter said. "Jim wanted to get to know you, to build up a certain level of trust. Then he planned to talk to you about us. He was almost ready to approach you. In another few days . . ."

Jillian grudgingly admitted that Jim had succeeded in gaining her trust. She'd liked him. She *had* trusted him—until his weird phone call. But approaching her in another way wouldn't have made a difference. If someone she loved, trusted, and respected told her the same story Jim had told and Roberta was telling, she wouldn't believe it. She didn't believe it.

"When the Beguiler arrived, Jim moved up his plan." Roberta sighed and sipped her coffee. "He feared for you. I'd almost say he panicked. He—"

"There were extenuating circumstances," Peter said, sounding indignant.

"Which Jillian need not concern herself with," Roberta snapped.

Peter gulped down some coffee, then folded his arms.

Jillian had the distinct impression that Roberta had just told Peter to shut up and that he wasn't happy about it. So far, she appeared to be the one in charge. Whether she was the top dog of this "cell" remained to be seen. Jillian bit into a piece of toast and waited for her to continue.

"I don't think Jim anticipated how strongly you'd resist the notion that our Lord has chosen you to carry out His work," Roberta said.

If she'd done her job right, and apparently she had, she'd come across as someone genuinely interested in spiritual matters. That aside, when Roberta had proclaimed where they'd find their next recruit, hadn't everyone else thought it a little convenient that their supposed Fledgling would drop into their lap at a quasi-religious service? It didn't take a rocket scientist to figure out that those most willing to join this . . . cult would be found in pews. Other information would be harder to come by. "How did Jim know who I was working for and what I was doing?" *Let me guess. The Lord told him—or Roberta.*

"Old-fashioned cyber-sleuthing," Roberta said.

Jillian grunted. It would take sophisticated equipment and a savvy operator to infiltrate the agency's system. Getting her cell phone number, a feat in itself, would have been child's play in comparison. "Why didn't Jim just drag me here when he concluded it was me?"

Roberta's forehead creased. "That's not the way we work. You must come willingly. We thought Jim could protect you until you were ready, but . . ." She sighed. "When he told us that he'd gone ahead and contacted you, and that you'd rebuffed him, we knew you'd tell Donaldson that Jim thought you were a Fledgling, but we didn't anticipate the speed or severity of his response. Well, not his response, exactly. He does what he's told."

"But I didn't tell Donaldson that Jim was looking for me," Jillian said.

"You didn't?" Roberta said sharply.

"No."

Peter and Roberta exchanged glances. "Then the Beguilers were just using her, and killing two birds with one stone," Peter breathed. "They didn't know she was the Fledgling. They must have tried to get it out of Jim." He grimaced. "That explains why they didn't capture her when she was at her mother's. They didn't know."

"They do now," Roberta said quietly.

Speaking of being at Mom's . . . "My mother and stepfather can vouch that I was with them. I've never understood why the police think I could have done it, when I wasn't even in town."

"The bodies were burned, Jillian," Peter said gently. "The police don't have an exact time of death. And Jim and Joanna were last seen before you left for your mother's. When they were actually killed . . ." He shrugged. "That's anybody's guess. Maybe before you left, maybe after. Either way, your visit to your mother's doesn't eliminate you."

Roberta tapped the table with her finger. "Jim was keeping an eye on you. He would have followed you to your mother's. As far as we know, he didn't. He last contacted us after he phoned you."

So he'd spied on her? She wasn't sure what bothered her more—that Jim had followed her around, or that she hadn't caught him doing it.

"They played their hand well," Peter said. "The police quickly fingering you as the prime suspect, the media oblivious until you were picked up . . . By the time we intercepted a police communication that gave us a hint of what was happening, it was too late to stop it."

"We did phone you," Roberta said, her mouth pinched.

How honest could she be? Would her seemingly benevolent hosts kill her if they feared that she'd expose them? She chuckled to herself. Who would she tell? The agency? The police? Life as she'd known it was over. "You have to understand that this all sounds far-fetched to me. I believe you're some sort of group. I believe you mean well. But I don't believe in God. I can't accept that I'm one of His," she waved her hand around, "Fledglings."

"You will in time," Roberta said firmly.

She wouldn't, but didn't see the point in arguing.

"We moved to plan B—breaking you out of prison, so to speak."

"That's where I came in." Peter smiled. "I think I did rather well, put in an award-winning performance. You believed I was a lawyer."

Jillian met his eyes. "You could have just told me you were the cavalry. I would have played dead."

His brows shot up. "Are you serious? Based on our dealings with you up to that point, we suspected that you'd shout for the guards, turn me in, and allow yourself to be railroaded into a life sentence."

She chuckled. "Point taken. But it was starting to sink in that I was in trouble, real trouble, and that nobody was going to help me." She held up her hand to forestall protests. "Meaning the agency. Donaldson." What about Keller? Had he just accepted that the woman he'd worked with for years was a murderer? Or had someone ordered him to stay out of it? "With life in prison stretching before me, I would have been more receptive to you." The circumstances would have dictated that she temporarily put aside her skepticism and listen, as she was now.

"We couldn't take that chance." Roberta's smile was strained. "You'd give doubting Thomas a run for his money."

Jillian almost smiled back, and hated herself for understanding the reference. God, she did speak their language, a fact that had become apparent when attending Jim's services and fundraising meetings. Almost sixteen years ago, she'd cast aside the religious life she'd lived and breathed from the moment she was born, yet slipping back into the mindset had been effortless. That alone was enough to frighten her, but it wasn't all. She'd felt more at home with Jim and his "flock" than she had with any of the other groups she'd wormed herself into over her career. It shouldn't feel so natural to sit here with religious fanatics, chuckling over doubting freaking Thomas. Enough chit-chat. "What happened after I passed out? Did I get bail?"

Roberta shook her head and pressed a button on the control panel. The botoxed face of the anchor on an all-news channel filled the screen. She yapped on about some problem in the Middle East. Jillian spooned more broth into her mouth, then went rigid with shock when the anchor said, "And now back to our top story of the day. Police are still hunting for Jillian Campbell, the woman accused in the Jim Preston double homicide." She cringed when her mug shot appeared on the screen. "Campbell was due in court this morning," the anchor said, over images of corrections officers escorting Jillian from the van to the courthouse's entrance, "but she collapsed at the courthouse. Armed men ambushed the ambulance carrying her to hospital, leaving many area residents shaken." An ambulance with its back doors wide open sat in an intersection, with police, and what looked like forensic experts, milling around it. "The lawyer who was with Campbell when she collapsed has also disappeared. Chief Williams had this to say at a press conference earlier today."

The police chief stood before a multitude of microphones. "An ambulance was called when a doctor at the courthouse couldn't revive her."

"What about the lawyer?" a reporter asked.

"We haven't found him yet."

"Was he involved?" another shouted.

"We don't know if he's an accomplice or a victim."

"Was anyone hurt?"

"No."

Now a bald man in a leather jacket filled the screen. "I was right on the corner," he said, pointing. "I heard the siren and stopped to look. I wondered why the ambulance slowed down, because it had a green light and the cop car in front had already gone through. Then the ambulance stopped, and the vans came out of nowhere. I couldn't believe it when a bunch of guys with machine guns jumped out."

"What happened then?" someone prompted from off screen.

"I don't know. When one of them looked at me, I ran."

"Why did the ambulance slow down?" Jillian asked.

Roberta turned off the TV. "Because I ordered the driver to," Peter said. "Since I had a gun pointed at his partner, he wasn't in a position to argue."

"You were in the ambulance with me?"

He nodded. "The police chief lied. The paramedics and the policeman riding with us know I'm an accomplice. So do the policemen who were escorting the ambulance. Plus, the identity we threw together for me wouldn't stand up under close scrutiny."

She could hardly believe her ears. "So let me get this straight. You claim you serve God, but you broke me out of prison using men with machine guns. What would you have done if the police or the paramedics had put up a fight? Shot them?"

"If we had to," Peter said, sending a chill up Jillian's spine.

"You're valuable, Jillian," Roberta said. "We would have done anything it took to bring you here, including shooting anyone who got in our way. We wouldn't have shot to kill, though."

Well, that was comforting. "Where is here?"

"Somewhere safe."

"And now what?" she said, deciding not to press Roberta for their exact location. "Whisking me away has made me look guilty. Are you going to help me clear my name? I'll be on every wanted list out there. I'm not going to be of much use to anyone, including you, unless we clear my name."

"We'll talk about that when Sam gets here."

Peter jerked his head toward Roberta. "You've called in Sam?"

"Someone has to train Jillian."

"We need to clear my name," Jillian said desperately. Or was that how they planned to control her? As long as she remained a wanted murderer, she couldn't leave, unless she wouldn't mind spending the rest of her life in prison.

"We'll talk about that later," Roberta said, her tone discouraging further argument. "For now, finish your broth."

"I wish I could call my mother," Jillian said, sure that Mom and Danny would be following the news of her escape. If they doubted her innocence, could she blame them?

Roberta nodded. "I think that can be arranged."

Chapter Six

WITH GRUDGING ADMIRATION, Jillian surveyed the equipment in the tech room and wondered who funded the group. Any doubts she had about Roberta's cyber-sleuthing explanation evaporated. They could hack into any system they wanted, though apparently they weren't spying on the house's occupants from here; the room lacked surveillance monitors. A separate security centre must exist, either in the house or on the grounds.

"This is Jeremy," Roberta said.

A twenty-something man swung his chair around and leaped to his feet. "So you're Jillian." She studied him. He sounded, but didn't look, familiar. Jeremy smiled, formed a fake phone receiver with his hand, and pressed it to his ear. "I'm trying to help you. We're trying to help you."

"That was you?"

He nodded and lowered his hand. "If you'd believed me, you would have saved us all a lot of trouble."

"At least I would have been conscious when I arrived," she said, suddenly feeling like a fly trapped in a spider's web. She'd thought she'd had a choice.

Roberta shot Jeremy a warning look. "We're happy you eventually made it here."

"Yes," Jeremy quickly agreed.

"Jillian wants to call her mother."

"Sure. I'll make sure they don't trace the call, but they might be listening in." He pursed his lips. "Even if they're not, I'm sure the police have told your mother to contact them if she hears from you, so be careful about what you say."

"I will." She wasn't an idiot.

"I'll leave you in Jeremy's hands, then," Roberta said. "When you're finished, join me in the library. Jeremy will bring you up. Sam should arrive soon."

"Yeah, she just landed," Jeremy said.

She?

"It's about five minutes from the airstrip to the house, so we won't have long to wait." Roberta turned to leave. "I'll see you upstairs."

Jeremy sat back down and motioned for Jillian to sit in a nearby office chair.

"So the call can't be traced?" Jillian asked. "Nope. Give me a second." While he typed away on his keyboard, she watched gibberish flash across the screen. He lifted a headset from the table and handed it to Jillian. "Put this on."

"My mother's number is—"

He held up his hand. "I've got it."

Of course he did. Jillian adjusted the headset's mouthpiece.

"Ready?"

"Yes."

He hovered his finger over a key. "When you're finished, hit this key, okay?" When she nodded, he hit the enter key.

One ring. Two rings. *Come on, Mom, pick up the phone.*

A click. "Hello?"

"Mom?"

"Jillian? Oh my god, where are you? Everyone's looking for you."

"It doesn't matter where I am," she said as Jeremy rose and left the room. "I just called to . . ." Say good-bye? No. "I wanted to tell you I didn't do it. I'm going to clear my name."

"Then why did you escape? I've seen the news. Who were those men? Why did you run away? If you didn't do it—"

"It's a long story. All I'll say is that I was pretty sure I wasn't going to get a fair trial."

"Jillian, this is crazy. Turn yourself in, okay? Turn yourself in. Oh my god, they might shoot you."

"Mom, I can't—"

"I couldn't deal with that. Not after your father. Turn yourself in. Please. I can't deal with—" Her voice choked off.

"Mom?" Shit, she could hear Mom crying.

Rustling noises, then, "Jillian?"

"I didn't do it, Danny."

"I know you didn't. I don't understand what the hell's going on, but I know you didn't do it."

She blinked back tears. "I didn't call to upset Mom, either." Her voice shook. She drew a deep breath. "I just wanted to let you know that I'm okay."

"You mean, you're not dead."

God, she loved this man and was so fortunate to have him in her life. "Listen, I'm going to clear my name. I won't be able to call again until I have." Her lips trembled. She gripped the arms of the chair. "Take care of her, Danny. And take care of—"

"Don't do this, sweetheart," he said quietly. "This isn't good-bye, all right? This isn't good-bye. You'll clear your name and then tell us all about it. Okay?"

"Okay," she managed to whisper. "I have to go."

"We love you."

"Good-bye." She pressed the disconnect key and ripped off the headset, then rubbed stray tears from her cheeks. That was it, then. Until she sorted out this mess, she was cut off from the only two people she trusted. She reluctantly rose and went into the hallway.

Jeremy was leaning against the wall, his arms folded. "You okay?"

She nodded. "Up to the library, I guess."

He pushed himself away from the wall. "Come on."

She fell into step with him and forced the phone call from her mind. She needed a clear head, especially when this Sam showed up.

"You're in good hands, you know," Jeremy said in the elevator. "I know you're skeptical and probably think we're all a bunch of deluded morons, but we're your best hope. We're on your side."

If he was trying to cheer her up, he'd failed miserably. Rather than muttering, "We'll see," she kept her mouth shut. She couldn't afford to antagonize them—not yet.

"Oh," Jeremy said when they entered the library. "Roberta's not here. I can keep you comp—"

"It's okay. I could use a quiet moment alone." She paused. "Unless you're worried I'll escape."

"You wouldn't get very far. See you at breakfast." He patted her arm and left.

Oh, great, community meals. Well, they couldn't let the one they were trying to bring into the cult have five minutes to herself, could they? Would they wake her up several times throughout the night, too? Nothing like a little sleep deprivation to open someone's mind. Once again, she felt trapped. Maybe sitting in a prison cell for the rest of her life would have been better. At least she'd know her mind was her own.

For now, she'd enjoy her solitude, and hoped her relief hadn't shown on her face when she and Jeremy had walked into an empty library. Jillian didn't feel comfortable around Roberta. What would Sam be like? She was supposedly one of these Deiforms. Jillian snorted softly and wandered over to one of the bookcases. This house was full of books. She ran her hand along the spines of numerous philosophy tomes, not the religion or theology books she'd expected. Those must be in another bookcase or room. Oh, here was a text she'd read for a college psychology—

"Hello, Jillian."

She spun around. The library was still empty.

"I'm pissed at you. Really pissed."

Roberta strolled into the library and frowned. "Are you all right?"

"Uh . . ."

"What's the matter?" Roberta asked, studying her.

She was hearing voices. Was it because Peter had drugged her? Her head hadn't felt quite right since she'd woken. Next time she saw him, she'd ask if hearing imaginary noises was a side effect of the drug wearing off. Was he still here? Her hands clenched. She didn't know the layout of the house, or how to find anybody.

"Jillian?"

"I'm fine," Jillian mumbled. "I'd like to speak to Peter."

"Are you sure you're all right?"

"Yes. I just want to ask him about—"

A woman marched into the room and stared at Jillian with contemptuous eyes. "So this is the one who cost us two people."

The woman's voice . . . Shock stabbed through Jillian.

Roberta stepped forward. "Sam . . ." she murmured.

Sam thrust out her hand. "Let me get this off my chest. If you expect me to work with her, let me get it off my chest." She planted herself right in front of Jillian, forcing her to shrink against the bookcase. "Jim and Joanna? They were my family. What dumb-ass goes to the person they've been warned against? Are you completely stupid? If it was up to me, you'd rot in prison."

"It's not up to you," Roberta said.

"Yes, she's out because of the God she doesn't believe in. Good for her." Sam blew out some air and shook her head, then jabbed her finger at Jillian. "You get any more of us killed and I don't give a shit what Roberta tells me to do. I'll make sure you pay. You got that?"

Jillian swallowed. "I didn't mean to get them killed," she said, mortified by her quavering voice. "I honestly didn't believe Jim's story. If I'd accepted that Donaldson was . . . working against you, I wouldn't have gone to him."

Sam blinked at her. "You'll find I'm not big on excuses," she said flatly.

"Give her a break, Sam," Roberta said. "You know Jim rushed it. We cautioned him, but he went ahead."

Jillian's shoulders slumped when Sam turned to Roberta. "When we found out who it was, you should have pulled him out," Sam said.

"I suggested sending someone else in, but he wanted to do it."

"You should have overruled him."

Roberta's chin came up. "Yes, I should have." The two women stared at each other for a moment, then Roberta held out her arms. "Welcome home."

While they embraced, Jillian tried to calm her racing heart. She couldn't wait to leave the library—and Sam.

"Let's sit," Roberta said.

Jillian dutifully sank into a chair. When Sam sat in the chair facing hers and glared, Jillian struggled to not shrink away. She twisted and focused on Roberta, who crossed her legs and smoothed her skirt.

"So, where are we?" Roberta said. "We became aware that a Fledgling was about to surface. We sent Jim to make contact. Jillian, you came to us, as we expected, but unaware, much to our surprise."

"Is that unusual?" Jillian asked.

"Yes, for two reasons. Usually we go to Fledglings and make contact, and usually they have some inkling of their gifts. At first we thought that perhaps Jim was wrong about you, but—"

"Jim wouldn't have made that mistake," Sam stated. "He wasn't wrong. But I understand why you initially questioned it."

"And once we were satisfied that Jillian—you," Roberta amended, glancing at Jillian, "were the one, we decided to wait and see if you'd become aware, but we obviously waited too long." Her eyes briefly closed. "And it cost us dearly."

Sam looked at Roberta. "At least we've got her. They didn't die in vain." She turned back to Jillian. "Yet."

Roberta nodded. "So now we train her and kill her."

Jillian's jaw dropped. "What?"

"You can't have any ties, Jillian. This is a life-long vocation that will require you to abide by God's law, not man's, and to forsake everyone and everything you know." Roberta leaned forward and raised her finger. "In this world, not of it. Everyone in this house is technically dead. If you were to look up our names, you'd find our obituaries. We need to create yours, and soon. The law is after you."

"Now, wait a minute," she sputtered. "Are you saying you're going to fake my death? That I'll never see my mother again? No!" She sliced her hand through the air for emphasis. "No way. Look, I don't have any of these gifts, whatever they are. Seriously. No inkling. None."

Roberta's brows shot up. "Nothing at all?"

"No. Nothing."

"You're lying!"

Sam's voice in her mind sounded as clear as her own. She scratched her nose and glanced surreptitiously at Sam, who appeared perfectly relaxed. Jillian shook herself. She really needed to see Peter. "That's why Jim's story sounded so insane. Why do you think I went to Donaldson? I thought Jim was trying to recruit me, to turn me against the agency. I'm not who you think I am. I don't want to join your fellowship."

"Let Sam work with you, and you'll quickly see that what we're telling you is true."

"And then you'll fake my death? No. If you think I'll die without clearing my name, you can think again. I'm not dying a double murderer. You got me into this mess. You can help me out of it." She folded her arms. "I'm not doing a damn thing until my name's cleared."

"You won't let us train you?"

"No."

Roberta and Sam stared at each other.

"You've got the wrong person," Jillian said desperately. "I'm hoping that by the time we've cleared my name, you'll see that."

"I wouldn't mind dealing with Donaldson," Sam said. "I know we usually don't retaliate, but he killed Jim and Joanna and framed an innocent. We can't look the other way on this one."

"If you're going after Donaldson, I'm in," Jillian said.

Roberta shifted her attention to Jillian. "So you agree that Donaldson is a threat?"

"I can accept that you're involved in something, he's opposed to whatever it is, and I'm caught in the middle, thanks to you. I don't accept the God stuff. I'm sorry, but I don't. I'll help you take down Donaldson, because the son of a bitch was having me locked away for the rest of my life." She paused to take a breath. "But once we're done dealing with him and clearing my name, we go our separate ways. Unless you're into kidnapping and holding someone against her will. Would your god condone that?"

Roberta's mouth pinched. "I know you're skeptical, but—"

"She's right," Sam said.

Roberta turned to her. "What?"

"She's right. Everyone comes willingly. She has to do the same. Let's take care of Donaldson and clear her name. If she wants to walk after that, let her walk. She won't last long, but it'll be her choice."

"We were instructed—"

"We were instructed to make contact. We've done that." Sam slid forward to perch on the edge of her chair. She met Roberta's eyes. "Trust Him. Let's do it her way and trust Him."

Roberta drew a deep breath and slowly exhaled. "All right."

"We'll start first thing in the morning. I need to go to the chapel." Sam rose and strode from the room, leaving behind an awkward silence.

"Can you take me to Peter?" Jillian asked. "And do you have a floor plan of the house? If I'm going to be here for a while, I don't want to have to bother you every time I want to see someone."

"Let me give you a tour." Roberta motioned for Jillian to follow her.

Jillian eagerly did, relieved that she'd be allowed to roam the house without an escort. She wouldn't meekly sit in her room. She'd find out everything she could about these people, to determine which side they were truly on, and what this whole religious shtick fronted. They were fighting a bad guy, but bad guys fought each other all the time.

JILLIAN PAUSED ON her way out of the conference room, where Peter had examined her again. "So you're sure the drug should have completely worn off by now."

"Yes." Peter removed his stethoscope and folded it. "But that doesn't mean you won't feel fatigued, or even a little woozy."

That wasn't what worried her. Hmm . . . didn't some people always hear noise? "What about tinnitus?"

"What about it?"

She grimaced. "Earlier on, my ears were ringing." Not entirely true, but close enough. Maybe she should just tell him that she'd heard voices. They were the crazy ones, not her.

Peter smiled reassuringly. "You're fine, Jillian. But I can understand why you might feel a little disoriented. Everything that's happened today . . . it's a lot to take in. A full night's sleep will do you good."

She lingered, still hoping for a rational explanation.

"Do you remember where your room is?" Peter asked, snapping his bag shut and lifting it from the table.

"Yes." Due to Roberta's tour, she had her bearings. "Her" room was the one she'd woken up in. "Thanks for checking me over."

"That's what I'm here for."

Jillian reluctantly left the sanest person in the house and called the elevator. Well, Jeremy hadn't claimed he could connect her to God in a couple of keystrokes. How had the two of them become mixed up with Roberta, Sam, and others in the Fellowship who believed they were divinely guided? Had they answered a job ad? Were they plucked from churches?

Turning the questions over in her mind, she stepped off the elevator on the second floor and walked down the hallway.

"I'm in your room. I hope you don't mind."

Shit. When she entered her bedroom, the sight of Sam gazing out the window didn't surprise her in the least—damn it!

Sam turned around and pointed at a duffel bag on the floor. "Clothes. Roberta asked me to pick some up for you. Nothing fancy. Jeans. T-shirts. Underwear. A couple of hoodies."

Jillian wouldn't give Sam the satisfaction of knowing that, when not working, she preferred jeans and t-shirts. Her jaw clenched. She'd bet that Sam already knew, and that every article of clothing in the bag was her size—including the freaking underwear. "Thanks," she mumbled.

"I heard Roberta gave you a tour."

Jillian nodded.

"After we figure out our first move tomorrow, I'll show you around outside."

"I'll look forward to being out of my cage for a bit."

"Nothing's stopping you from leaving the house now. Go ahead. Stumble around in the dark."

"Nobody will come after me?"

"No."

Nonplussed, Jillian stared at her. "I didn't think I'd be allowed to roam freely outside. Aren't you worried that I'll escape?"

Sam snorted. "Unless you can swim long distances, fly a plane, or sail a large boat on your own, you won't get very far."

The lightbulb came on. "We're on an island," Jillian stated. "Not that it matters. I have nowhere to go. I'm an escaped murder suspect, remember?"

Sam grunted. "There's that, too."

"Can I ask you a question?"

"Sure."

"Roberta said I'm valuable. She said you would have done whatever it takes to bring me here. But after we've brought down Donaldson, you're willing to let me walk. Why?"

"Because I know you won't walk," Sam said firmly.

"You don't know me."

"I know what you are. That's enough."

Jillian seethed at the woman's arrogant and smug attitude. "I'm not a Fledgling."

"Yes, you are."

Shit!

"While we're clearing your name, we have to trust each other." Sam's eyes bored into Jillian. "Step number one is to stop lying to me."

"I'm not lying to you."

Sam raised a finger. "Jillian, stop lying to me. You can hear me."

"No, I—"

"Stop. Lying. To me." *"Stop it!"*

Jillian grabbed her head with both hands. "Look, I was drugged, okay? I'm not quite myself."

"And Peter agreed that the drug might be causing whatever you're denying?" When Jillian remained silent, Sam said, "I didn't think so. Let me take a crack at describing what you're hearing. My voice. Inside your head. How am I doing?"

Too damn well. "Yeah, I suppose that sort of describes the after-effect of the drug." When Sam chuckled, Jillian wanted to throttle her. Screw this. "How are we going to bring down Donaldson and clear my name?"

Sam's eyes narrowed. "I'll—we'll think about that once we've seen what Jeremy has dug up. Why don't you get some sleep?"

Because she'd rather work on getting her life back. The sooner they accomplished their goal, the sooner she'd be out of here. But this was their game, and she needed a clear head. "Good idea."

"We're meeting in the conference room after breakfast."

"Okay."

"Oh, there's a toothbrush in the bag, along with a comb, deodorant, the usual."

"Thanks." She'd visit the bathroom, then see if Sam had also included pajamas or a nightie.

"Good night." Sam headed for the door.

"Sam."

She turned around.

"I'm sorry about Jim and Joanna."

Sam's face froze. After a second, she nodded. "Thank you." Then she leaned against the doorframe. "I know this is all a bit sudden for you. You're not sure whether you've fallen in with a bunch of criminals, or a bunch of crazies, and words won't sway you either way. You'll let this play out and draw your own conclusions."

Sam's accurate assessment of Jillian's thoughts and intentions took her by surprise. "I'm not trying to be difficult. I just—"

"I get it, especially since you're being honest about not having any inkling, at least not before today. You're also older than usual. Most Fledglings come in when they're in their early twenties."

"How old were you?"

"Nineteen."

If Jillian had estimated Sam's age correctly, they were both in their thirties. That would mean . . .

"Almost twenty years ago," Sam said, reading the question in Jillian's eyes . . . or maybe her mind!

"Roberta mentioned gifts. What sort of—"

"You'll have plenty of opportunity to ask questions." Sam pushed away from the doorframe. "Get some sleep. Good night."

This time, Jillian didn't call her back. As she rummaged through the duffel bag for the toothbrush and other toiletries, her mind burst with questions. How had Sam discovered she was a Fledgling? How had the Fellowship contacted her? How had Sam "died?" What exactly did she do for the Fellowship?

Listen to me! After one short conversation with Sam, she sounded like she believed this crap. Surrounded by people who did believe it, or damn good actors, she needed to be on her guard. Plenty of time together also meant plenty of time to play with her mind, to indoctrinate her. This whole setup had the whiff of a cult. If she wasn't careful, she'd be on this island for the rest of her life—willingly.

Chapter Seven

A S SHE LISTENED to the others weigh in on her predicament, Jillian resisted the urge to pinch herself. After sleeping soundly through the night, she felt much better this morning. Nobody had shaken her awake at regular intervals, depriving her of a restful sleep, and she hadn't heard Sam's voice in her mind since last night. Now that her head was clear, she wondered how much of yesterday had been real. She hadn't hallucinated the basic events that had taken place in this house, but the weird stuff . . . and hearing Sam in her mind . . . had it really happened? Yesterday had the aura of a dream about it; today felt grounded in reality. The conversation around her sounded surreal only because of its topic.

Sitting across from Jillian, Sam leaned back in her chair and laced her fingers behind her head. "Jim was right. Donaldson wanted to use someone he could easily discredit. Then, when they decided to go after Jim and kill him . . ." Her voice lost some of its vigour, and she heaved her shoulders. "They used her again, not only to take the rap, but to lock away a person who knew about their existence."

As if she would have told anyone about what Jim had said regarding the Beguilers. She liked to come across as a sane human being, thank you very much.

Roberta gave Sam a long look. "That was quite the coincidence, wasn't it? Donaldson wants to find out why Jim has surfaced and is staying visible, so he sends in Jillian, the Fledgling Jim is waiting for?"

"I don't believe in coincidences," Sam said. "If Donaldson hadn't sent Jillian to Jim, she never would have come to us. You saw, sensed—however you do it—a Fledgling coming to us at a service.

You saw business people, a meeting room, an informal gathering, but definitely a spiritual one. Jillian would never have attended such a meeting on her own initiative. Someone had to send her."

Startled, Jillian reached for her tea and gave Sam a surreptitious glance.

"When we figured out that she worked for Donaldson, I knew right away that he didn't know about her," Sam continued. "If he had, he would have had his answer. He wouldn't have had a reason to use her."

"Wait." Jillian set her cup in its saucer. "You knew about Donaldson before any of this happened?"

"Yes, but he didn't know that we knew." Roberta's voice dropped. "Until you told him."

Jillian's heart sank. It didn't matter how crazy it all sounded. If not for her, two people might still be alive. "Sorry. I—"

Roberta held up her hand. "We've gone through this already."

Jeremy, who hadn't said more than two words since the meeting began, piped up. "When we found out about him, we decided to keep him in play, so we'd know when he became interested in one of our projects. We sometimes invented situations for him to investigate, to distract him from what we actually cared about."

"We're not sure if the Beguilers put Donaldson into that position, or if they pursued him because of his position," Roberta said. "Either way, it was a brilliant move on their part. Not everything we care about comes to Donaldson's attention, but some of it does."

"It was brilliant until we noticed a pattern and fingered him." The pride in Jeremy's voice led Jillian to suspect that he'd uncovered Donaldson's association with the Beguilers.

"When they found out Jim was looking for a Fledgling, they must have decided to go after him," Roberta said, as Sam gave Jeremy a thumbs up, confirming Jillian's suspicion.

"They couldn't resist," Sam said quietly. "The fact that you ended up in prison, rather than dead, means Jim died without giving them what they wanted."

Apparently, breaking her out had tipped off the Beguilers that she was the one. "Maybe you should have left me in prison."

Sam shook her head. "You're too valuable to leave in prison, and you would have been vulnerable. If they'd eventually figured out that you're the Fledgling, they would have visited and tried to turn you to them. They might have succeeded. What were the chances that Jillian Campbell would find the Lord in prison?"

Jillian snorted. "I always figure that convicts who convert in prison quickly lose their faith once they're out." The second the words were out of her mouth, she wanted to take them back. She was at the mercy of these people. Ridiculing and insulting their views was risky. "I wouldn't have gone over to their side. I'd have had as much trouble accepting their . . . beliefs as I do yours."

"Don't kid yourself. You would have lapped up everything they were offering. They would have known what buttons to press."

Jillian glared at her. "I'm not a helpless, suggestible idiot, you know. I do have a brain."

Sam's mouth tightened. "I never said you didn't. They're master manipulators, and they would have had all the time in the world. Of course, they might have decided to just kill you and be done with it." She rested her elbows on the table and clasped her hands together. "Anyway, this is all very interesting, but there's no way we would have left you in prison." She turned to Roberta and Jeremy. "What's our next move? We need to clear her name so we can start training her."

Jillian wanted to punch the woman. She was not staying here, damn it!

"Did you get your hands on the police files?" Roberta asked Jeremy.

He nodded. "I thought maybe they'd be purged, but they're still there."

"Of course they're still there," Roberta said. "Our swift action has put our opponents into a bit of a pickle. They involved the police by framing her. It's all over the news. They can't make the investigation go away, not with two bodies, an escaped suspect, and every police organization in the world on the lookout for her."

Terror gripped Jillian. This wasn't a dream. She couldn't decide she'd had enough, bid them all good-bye, and go home. Without their protection, she'd be back in a cell and convicted of a double murder.

"We want to clear her name and punish Donaldson, right?" Sam said. "So here's what I propose . . . We prove that Donaldson set her up, that he intended all along to kill Jim and Joanna, and that's why he put her on the case. She was always going to be his scapegoat for murder."

"And how the hell are you going to do that?" Jillian asked. "Especially since you know it's not true. He didn't intend it all along." The bastard had improvised when she'd gone running to him.

Sam narrowed her eyes. "Did you kill Jim and Joanna?"

"No!"

"Yet they have reams of evidence showing that you did."

Jillian drew breath, then nodded.

"I like it," Roberta said. "It has a certain elegance to it."

"Yeah, I'm glad it'll take down Donaldson, too." Sam drummed her fingers on the table. "We can't make it too obvious. Let's figure out what trail we'll lay. Once we have that, we'll work out how to shine a light on it. Jeremy, create an itemized list of every shred of evidence they have."

Jeremy shifted in his chair. "I had a quick look at the files. The case is air-tight. If I didn't *know* she didn't do it, I'd believe she did. This won't be easy."

"We'll find a way," Sam said. "I'm going to show Jillian around the grounds. We'll get started as soon as we come back."

"Okay." Jeremy rolled back his chair.

Sam followed suit and looked at Jillian. "You coming?"

In response, Jillian downed the rest of her tea and pushed away from the table. Apprehensive and filled with questions, she followed Sam from the room.

WHEN SAM POINTED to a large flat rock near the shore and suggested that they sit for a bit, Jillian enthusiastically agreed. After keeping up with Sam for over an hour as they toured part of the island, she was ready for a breather. Raven and Puck had wandered around with them for a while, but had suddenly bounded away together. "They're going back to the house," Sam had murmured. Maybe they had a routine.

Jillian sank down next to Sam, stretched out her legs, and gazed out at the calm water. With the sun warming her face, she imagined herself rolling her hoodie into a makeshift pillow and curling up for a nap. Hard to believe she was on the run from the law. "It's so peaceful."

Sam grunted.

Jillian squinted at her. Not wanting to irritate the woman too soon and bring an abrupt end to their time together, she'd bitten back her questions while Sam showed her around. But they were bursting to come out. If she didn't badger Sam now, she might not get another opportunity before they returned to the others. "So what are these gifts Roberta mentioned?"

"I thought you didn't want to be trained," Sam said.

"I don't. I'm curious."

Sam brushed a twig off her jeans. "Since you won't train, I can't tell—"

Jillian leaped to her feet. "Come on, Sam, give me something! I'm stumbling around in the dark, here. You want me to accept everything you say at face value. I can't do that. This time last week, I was leading my normal hum-drum life. Now I'm an escaped suspect in a double murder, being harboured by a group that claims to work for God and expects me to just trust it. See it from my point of view!"

Sam looked up at her. "Are you usually this . . . excitable?"

"Only when I'm on the lam." Her frustration eased when Sam chuckled.

"Sit down," Sam said.

Jillian hesitated, then lowered herself down and drew her legs to her chest. "Would you have to swim to the mainland, or could you walk there?" Her blood pressure shot up again when Sam laughed. "Come on! Why won't you tell me anything? Are you afraid I'll figure out it's a load of bull?"

The amusement in Sam's eyes faded. "The less you know, the better."

"Why? What harm would telling me do? What would I do with the information?"

"It's more about what the Beguilers might do to you."

Jillian frowned at her.

Sam sighed. "They know you're here, and they'll assume you've accepted your purpose and we're training you, which means they only have a small window of opportunity to try to kill you."

"What do you mean?"

"If they can get to Fledglings before we do, they try to turn them. If they can't turn them, they kill them. If they can't get to a Fledgling in time, they wait until the freshly trained Deiform leaves the protection of the cell. Then they strike. Because taking down a seasoned Deiform is next to impossible."

"What about Jim?"

Sam fell silent for a moment. "Jim worries me. Even most green Deiforms can defend against an attack. The Beguilers try anyway because a slim chance is the best chance they'll ever get. In your case . . . you won't stand a chance."

Jillian swallowed. "I'll tell them I didn't train, that you wanted me to, but I walked away."

"They won't believe you, especially when you tell them all about the gifts. They already know about some of them, but they'll make you tell them, anyway, and have fun doing it. Maybe if you can't tell them, no matter how hard they push . . . I don't know . . ." Sam's eyes were bleak.

So Sam wouldn't divulge all her secrets because of the miniscule possibility that the Beguilers wouldn't harm her if she remained clueless? "I thought you said they'd kill me. When would I have a chance to tell them anything?"

"They'll kill you, all right. They'll capture you, and then they'll take their time, draw it out and enjoy it. If you can't tell them about the gifts, no matter what they do to you, maybe they'll show you some mercy and give you a quick death. Or maybe they'll get angry."

She shuddered. "I want my life back!"

Sam turned to her. "You lost your life the moment you walked into the community centre that first time," she said softly. "It doesn't matter whether you believe that or not. It's the truth. I'm sorry."

Sam's apology and sincere tone frightened Jillian.

"I'll tell you more about what you already know, but that's it." Sam smiled weakly. "Deal?"

Jillian quickly nodded. She'd take any tidbits Sam was willing to throw her.

"Okay. You know that I can telepathically communicate with you." She paused, perhaps waiting for Jillian to deny it, but Sam's honesty and willingness to meet her halfway made her want to be honest in return. Maybe they were drugging her food. Maybe Peter had lied about the after-effects of whatever he'd given her. Maybe there was something physically wrong with her, or stress was causing her to hear voices that weren't there. For this conversation, she'd assume it was real. "We can communicate with other Deiforms—and Fledglings—that are within a certain range," Sam continued.

"What range?"

Sam considered the question. "Maybe a hundred feet or so."

"That's not much."

"You'd be surprised how incredibly useful it can be when Deiforms are working together."

"Can you read the minds of other Deiforms—and Fledglings?" Fervently hoping the answer would be no, she was relieved when Sam shook her head. "Why not?"

Sam shrugged. "I don't know. At first I thought maybe it had to do with invasion of privacy, but—"

"But . . ."

"I can't tell you."

There must be another gift that did invade privacy. "Jim mentioned something about sensing Beguilers."

"Yes, we can do that, too."

"Can they sense you?"

"No."

"What abilities do they have?"

"They can twist your mind, make you see things that aren't real. If you ever run into one . . ." She shook her head. "It's almost impossible to know when it's happening to you. That's about it for their abilities."

Jillian took a moment to digest the information. "I'm getting the impression that you're more powerful than they are, so why don't you just obliterate them and be done with it?"

Sam's mouth turned up at the corners. "First, new Beguilers would come forth. Second, our purpose isn't to defeat them. It's to act as our Lord's agents."

"I don't have a clue what you mean."

"When our Lord instructs a Guide to look into a situation, we do. Sometimes, but not always, the Beguilers have an interest in, or even initiated, whatever situation we're investigating. Our Lord's opponent is a meddler, a trickster, a tempter. He's always trying to corrupt, manipulate, incite, interfere with our Lord's plan. His Beguilers can be clever. But overall, we manage to stay ahead. Sometimes we act proactively to do so."

"So you're here to keep them in check."

"Not primarily. As I said, what we investigate may or may not have anything to do with the Beguilers. Unfortunately, they hardly ever pass up an opportunity to turn or kill a Fledgling. They rarely try to take out a seasoned Deiform, though. That's why Jim's death is shocking on a number of levels." Sam averted her gaze and rubbed her nose.

Jillian felt compelled to express her condolences again, but knew it wouldn't help, especially when Sam might be trying hard to not hold her responsible for Jim and Joanna's deaths.

Sam stared out at the horizon. "That's all I can tell you," she finally said.

Jillian had gleaned new information from the conversation, but not much about the gifts—exactly what Sam wanted. "Thanks for telling me what you can."

"I can teach you how to do what I can do. All you have to do is commit to us. It would get the law off your back, too. They close cases when the suspect dies. It would save us the trouble of framing Donaldson."

She opened her mouth to sharply retort, then thought better of it. "Would you want to die a double murderer? Because everyone's already convicted me." Except perhaps Mom and Danny. "And that would mean Donaldson gets away with it. With everything."

"Oh, we'd still deal with Donaldson." Sam paused. "You shouldn't worry about what people think. You should only care about what the Lord thinks. He knows you're innocent."

Jillian took a deep, calming breath before responding. "I don't believe in God. And I don't want to clear my name for me, not entirely. I want to do it for my mother. She's already been to hell and back. She's not going there again because I'm caught up in a battle that's not mine." She met Sam's eyes and refused to look away. She was doing her best to respect Sam's views. Sam had better respect hers, damn it!

After seconds that felt like minutes, Sam said, "Your own words betray you. You would fit in here just fine."

Jillian blinked.

Sam pulled a phone from her pocket, punched a key, and put the phone to her ear. "You ready yet? Good, we're coming back. We'll meet you in the conference room."

"Jeremy?" Jillian said as she followed Sam's lead and stood.

Sam nodded. "It's time to clear your name."

Chapter Eight

Reeling over the evidence Jeremy had presented, Jillian stared down at her notes. It wasn't the first time she'd heard the bulk of the case against her, but she'd sat in shock when Trotter had filled her in, her brain refusing to accept the impossible. Hearing and seeing it a second time . . . She'd remained quiet while Sam and Jeremy batted around ideas about how to counter each piece of evidence in ways that pointed to Donaldson. Every photo, statement, and forensic report had dealt a blow to her spirits and driven home the stark reality that she was in deep, deep shit.

Donaldson, or the Beguilers, had strung her up thoroughly. If the police recaptured her, she wouldn't leave prison until she was old and gray—if she survived. According to Sam, her life would be in peril the moment she left the island. If the Beguilers did consider her a threat, for whatever reason, then she was doomed.

Even if the Fellowship successfully framed Donaldson, she wouldn't join it. Regardless of what she thought of them and their views, she had principles. If she pretended that she believed in God to save her own skin, she'd hate herself. Every time she looked in the mirror, she'd see a weak, pathetic woman who'd sold her integrity because she was afraid to die. She didn't want to die a double murderer; she didn't want to live as a hypocrite. She was screwed. Utterly and completely screwed.

Her only hope was that everything Sam had said about the Beguilers' interest in her was bullshit. But the prospect that Sam had deliberately lied to her didn't sit well. Her gut told her that Sam sincerely believed she acted on behalf of God. It wasn't a cover story for criminal activities, or a yarn meant to manipulate Jillian into joining some weird cult. Well, people who saw things honestly believed those things were there, right? If Sam was deluded, she believed her delusion. Still, Jillian was inclined to trust her. Hell, if Sam's make-believe world got her out of this mess, all the more power to it!

For a moment, she considered the possibility that she was actually in a psychiatric institution. Maybe she'd had a mental breakdown, and whatever drugs they were pumping into her had created this alternate reality—it was *her* make-believe world, and not Sam's; Sam didn't exist. Peter could be a doctor in the real world, her only connection to reality. She hadn't seen him since last night. Jim calling her could have been an illusion, her first break with reality as her sanity began to deteriorate.

Nah. Everything felt so real that, if she accepted her theory, she'd have to question reality from this point forward. She was perfectly sane, and sitting here, at this table, with real people. Real people with weird views, but real people, all the same. As Sam had said, she'd see how it played out and hope she had a life to return to when the dust settled; hopefully there'd be one in which she wasn't constantly looking over her shoulder.

Motion in her peripheral vision snapped her back to her surroundings. Jeremy stood looking at her. "What would you like?" he asked.

"What?"

"For lunch. What type of sandwich?"

"He's going to get us lunch. While he's gone, we'll move on to the next item," Sam said, to Jillian's surprise. Considering she'd contributed next to nothing so far, she would have expected Sam to suggest that they break until Jeremy returned.

"A tuna sandwich, if you can," she said. "If not, egg, cheese, salmon. Anything but peanut butter. Can't stand the stuff."

"One tuna sandwich, coming up," Jeremy said with a grin. He left without asking Sam what she wanted. She must have already told him, or he was familiar with her eating habits. Jillian wondered what he'd bring for her.

Sam got up and closed the door. Before sitting back down, she lifted a sheet from the evidence pile and slid it across the table to Jillian. "Let's talk about that."

Jillian looked down and read it. Blood rushed to her cheeks. It was the semen and hair report. She lifted her head. Sam had sat down and clasped her hands on the table. "Is it real, or was it planted?"

"I can't believe you're asking that," Jillian sputtered. "Do you honestly think—"

"Normally I'd say that if you and Jim were having a sexual relationship, that's your business," Sam said, though her expression suggested that she wouldn't condone such a relationship. "We might not try to counter this particular evidence. It's not key to the case, and we've already come up with enough rope to hang Donaldson. But I want to know if Jim was distracted, if something was going on that made him vulnerable."

Jillian gritted her teeth and suppressed her indignation. "We weren't sleeping together, I swear. Not only was he old enough to be my father, but he wasn't my type. I didn't even spend much time alone with him. I mainly worked with Mike."

"I figured, but I wanted to make sure." Sam shrugged apologetically. "When we researched your background, romantic relationships were notably absent."

Excuse me? "How about I go over every minute of your entire freaking life and see how you like it? I'm sure ten minutes in Jeremy's room would be very enlightening."

"Not really. All you'd find out is that I was a model child and student, and died when I was nineteen." Sam grimaced. "And that's if anyone tells you my last name. I don't think 'Sam' will get you very far."

Jillian's jaw clenched. "Can we get back to the evidence? Because I'd really like to clear my name and get the hell out of here."

"Sure."

God, Sam irritated the crap out of her! "As for my background, there's no point getting involved with anyone when my identity changes every five minutes." She hated herself for wanting to explain, but at least she wasn't telling Sam everything. She was certain they hadn't discovered she was a lesbian when they'd snooped through her life. Not only had she spent her life in the closet, but they would have brought it up by now. Maybe she should tell them. If she was lucky, they'd throw her off the island . . . and right into the hands of the law. Nope, clear her name, then burn the bridges.

"That's convenient for you, isn't it?" Sam raised her brows. "Constantly changing lives, so you can avoid living."

Jillian bit her tongue. "I want this countered," she said, tapping the sheet in front of her. "I don't care that it's not key to the case. I don't know who's seen this."

"It matters to you that people might think you were sleeping with Jim."

"Of course it matters! If—when—I'm exonerated, I could lose my job. You don't sleep with the person you're investigating, or at least you don't for the types of cases I work. It would be completely unprofessional—and stupid."

Sam drew breath.

"Please don't say I shouldn't be worrying about my job because I won't be going back to it."

"Actually, I was going to say that it'll be easy to counter. Someone could have taken a bed sheet from Jim's place, put it on your bed, and added, uh, traces of you from your sheet."

"Do we have a photo of the sheet that was on my bed?"

Sam sifted through a pile of photos, pulled one out, and passed it across the table to Jillian.

She peered at it. "I can't tell if it's mine or not. It's the same plain old blue sheet that millions of people have on their beds." Wait. "Someone did replace my sheet! I own a blue sheet like this, but I had a green sheet on the bed."

"Don't get too excited. Like I said, this isn't key to their case. In fact, all it does is suggest that you and Jim had more than a professional relationship. It supports their theory. It doesn't make their case."

"Yeah, even without it, I'm still screwed." Jillian chuckled. "Bad word choice."

Sam didn't smile.

"How long do you think it'll take to clear my name?"

"Setting up Donaldson and pulling the trigger?"

Jillian nodded.

"I don't know. Jeremy can plant most of the evidence from here, but not all of it. I'll take care of what he can't do, which shouldn't be much, but we can't put the plan into motion until Jeremy's ready. And we haven't quite figured out how to bring the evidence to light in a way that doesn't look suspicious. So . . . a few days, maybe? A week?"

And she was expected to sit around with her life hanging in the balance, while Sam and Jeremy did whatever they needed to do. Great. "I don't suppose there's any way I can help you."

"No."

"The waiting will drive me crazy."

"I'll keep Roberta updated."

Jillian frowned.

"I won't be gone long."

Jillian didn't care if Sam would only be gone an hour; it would feel like an eternity.

"Trust me," Sam said.

"I do. But I'm not a sit on my hands type of person. I'm used to taking care of myself. I'm not good at waiting." She sighed, then brightened. "Take me with you."

Sam's eyes bulged. "Are you nuts? Have you already forgotten the conversation we had outside?"

No, but she wasn't worried about being pursued and killed because she was a Fledgling. How could she be, when she didn't believe any of it? She was only in this mess because thugs had framed her. Sam believed the Beguilers would hunt her down, but why would they, when Jillian wasn't a threat to them? The police concerned her more, but if she changed her appearance and holed up in a motel or wherever Sam stayed when she wasn't here . . . "I won't be alone, fending for myself. I'll be with you. Take me with you. At least I'll be . . ." She searched for the right words. "I'll feel as if I'm doing something, instead of sitting around. I can research stuff for you."

"Jeremy can do that."

"Okay, bounce ideas around with you, if you run into a problem. Make you dinner. Do your laundry. I don't know, anything. Take me with you."

"No."

"Please?"

"No!"

"NO!" SAM SHOUTED. "Absolutely not."

Roberta stood up and glared at her.

Eyeing the two women from her chair in the library and trying not to gloat, Jillian hoped Roberta would stand her ground. She'd been as surprised as Sam when Roberta had brought it up, but for her, the surprise was a pleasant one. For Sam . . .

Sam's hands went to her hips. "We broke her out and brought her here because she's a Fledgling. Now you want to put her in harm's way?"

"We broke her out and brought her here so she could be trained, and I called you here to train her." Roberta sounded calm, but her eyes blazed. "You're the one who said no, let's do it her way. Let's respect her choice. In fact, I believe you said that after we've cleared her name, if she wants to go, let her go. She'll be in danger, but it's her choice."

Sam huffed. "I said to trust Him. She'll train."

"Trust Him doesn't mean it'll just work itself out. What are you expecting will happen, that she'll be hit by a lightning bolt while you're gone and suddenly agree to train?" Roberta pointed at Jillian. "How is she supposed to make an informed choice, to truly understand what we do, if all she's going to do is wait here until you tell her it's safe to go home? She'll be with you. You can protect her."

"No." Shaking her head, Sam turned to pace. "No way."

"Jeremy and I have an idea about how she can play a role in bringing our evidence to light."

"We'll find another way."

Roberta's nostrils flared. "She needs to see it, Sam. How else will she come around? I don't like it, either. I'd rather she stay on the island, but since you refuse to train her until she accepts her purpose, we'll have to risk it." Her brow furrowed. "Or perhaps not. I'm going to call in Warren to train her, whether she wants to train or not."

Jillian opened her mouth to protest, then promptly closed it when Roberta shot her a warning look and curtly shook her head.

"Unless you take her with you," Roberta continued. "Otherwise there's no chance she'll agree to train, as far as I'm concerned. Nothing will change for her while she's here."

Sam swung back to Roberta. "Go ahead. Call in Warren and try to train her. It won't work. Not with her."

"Then she needs to see more. Can't you understand that?"

"I was hoping to protect her. The more she knows—"

"You say she'll ultimately train, but you're behaving as if she'll walk away. I'm going to say your words back to you. Trust Him. Have faith. Act as if you believe she'll remain. Act as if you *know*."

Sam stared at the floor, then let out a long, exasperated sigh and pivoted toward Jillian. "Be ready to leave tomorrow morning at eight." The bookcases shook as she marched from the room.

Roberta sank into her chair and ran a hand through her hair as she slowly exhaled. She turned to Jillian. "You endanger her in any way, and I'll see that you're punished. Do you understand?"

Jillian understood that, by "punished," Roberta meant more than a stern word. She'd literally rip the eyeballs from Jillian's head.

"You follow Sam's directions. You do exactly what she tells you to do. If you want to argue with her, save it until you're both safely back here."

Jillian wanted to scream, but settled for clenching her hands on her lap. "I'm not coming back, Roberta. I won't do anything to hurt Sam, I promise. I want to help her clear my name. I need her." She also felt an affinity for Sam that she didn't feel for anyone else here. Roberta came across as aloof, and Jillian still didn't have a handle on what Roberta's "duties" were and whether she was in charge. Peter seemed to have disappeared—maybe he'd left the island. And when Jeremy wasn't in a meeting, he preferred his computers to human conversation. Earlier, Jillian had met Emma, another techie who apparently worked the night shift. She'd probably never see her again. Nope, she'd rather take her chances with Sam than twiddle her thumbs and watch the clock. "But once we've cleared my name, I'm picking up the pieces of my life—out there."

Roberta studied her. "We'll see," she murmured, then changed the subject before Jillian could retort. "We're holding a service for Jim and Joanna tonight. Don't feel you have to attend. We value honesty over hypocrisy."

"What time?"

"Seven."

"I'll pay my respects in my own way. It'll still be light outside. I'll go for a walk, perhaps visit the graveyard Sam showed me."

"Jim's remains belong in that graveyard. It's unfortunate we can't bury them here, but they're just bones. Jim has moved on." Roberta stared down at her lap. "Have you visited the chapel since you arrived?"

"No," Jillian said flatly.

"It contains some wonderful pieces." Roberta lifted her head. "The stained glass is exquisite."

Jillian grunted.

Roberta's face tightened, but she didn't pursue it further. "We'll have to do something about your appearance. Jeremy is working on ID. He'll need a new photo of you."

Unless Jeremy was psychic—not out of the question in this place!—Roberta had set him to work on creating an identity before she'd persuaded Sam to take Jillian with her. Had Roberta intended to send her off the island with Sam ever since that first conversation in the library? Tension existed between those two. Why?

"Meet me here at 8:30 tonight," Roberta said.

"Okay. If there's nothing else, I'll go read." She was in the middle of a good mystery she'd found in a bookcase in the study. Unfortunately, that was all she'd discovered. She'd poked around in just about every room except the bedrooms and Jeremy's cave. Nothing. If there was anything incriminating to be found, it was in one of the other buildings on the island, and she didn't have access to those. Many were houses with inhabitants Sam had declined to identify.

"I'll see you later, then." Roberta reached for the lemonade on the table next to her chair.

Desperate to leave, Jillian strode from the library, descended the stairs to the second floor, and strode along the hallway to her bedroom, where the mystery book lay on the bed. She slowed her pace as she passed the closed door to Sam's room. Sam must be furious. While Jillian was pleased that she wouldn't be stuck on the island wondering how the operation was progressing, she hoped Roberta's order hadn't turned Sam against her. She hadn't liked Sam's refusal to take her, but she'd accepted it. She wouldn't have pushed. But now wouldn't be the right time to try to appease Sam; she'd let her calm down first. Jillian picked up her pace and continued down the hallway.

Chapter Nine

Jillian shifted her weight as she waited with Roberta for Sam to come downstairs. She hadn't seen Sam since the blow-up in the library, and apprehensively gazed up the stairs when the floor overhead creaked. A moment later, Sam came down the winding staircase, a bag slung over her shoulder. She eyed Jillian, then shifted her attention to Roberta and dropped her bag to the floor. "I think I like her better as a brunette."

Roberta chuckled and held out her arms. "Be careful," she said as she hugged Sam. She sounded genuinely concerned, and Sam's return embrace was tight. Maybe the tension between the two was nothing more than that experienced between members of any family: they had their disagreements but loved each other.

Roberta drew back and reached for Jillian, who hesitated, then hugged her. The gesture felt awkward. She wasn't a touchy-feely person who manhandled acquaintances. Hell, she couldn't remember the last time she'd hugged her mother and Danny. She quickly pulled away from Roberta and hoped she didn't look too uncomfortable.

"I'll look forward to welcoming you into the fold when you return," Roberta said.

Jillian pressed her lips together.

Roberta raised a finger. "As soon as you've cleared up this mess, bring her back," she said to Sam. "I don't want her off this island a second longer than she has to be."

"Don't worry, I agree," Sam said. "In fact, I would have preferred that she not leave the island at all. But, no matter," she quickly added, having made her point. She picked up her bag. "Let's go."

Jillian lifted the bag at her feet and followed Sam out the front door. Gravel crunched underfoot as they walked to a four-door Jeep. After they'd stored their bags in the back, Jillian slid into the passenger seat and fastened her seatbelt.

Sam turned the key in the ignition. "Airstrip's not far away," she said, stepping on the accelerator.

Hoping for a mirror, Jillian pulled down the visor. *Yes!* As she had in the bathroom that morning, she examined her new look. "Do you think this'll fool everyone?"

"It'll fool the casual observer, which is all we really care about. Even if you were to pass someone who knows you, they probably wouldn't notice it's you. You'd have to speak to them." Sam paused. "I'd know it's still you, though."

"How?"

"You still have that 'I think they're all nuts' look in your eyes."

Jillian snorted. "You know, if not for the fact that you're bat-shit crazy, I could seriously like you." When Sam remained silent, she worried that she'd gone too far and scrambled for something conciliatory to say that wouldn't make things worse.

"This bat-shit crazy person is responsible for keeping you safe," Sam said while Jillian was still flailing. "I guess Roberta's hoping that you'll see some of my gifts in action and decide we're not so crazy after all, but I don't like it. I would have preferred to bring you around in a way that doesn't involve putting you in danger."

"I didn't ask Roberta to force you into bringing me along, if that's what you think. As for a less risky way, I asked you to tell me about . . . your gifts. If you'd done that, shown me . . ."

Sam gave her a sidelong glance, then turned her attention back to the gravel road. "You wouldn't have wanted to come along?"

"Well, no, I still would have."

"You would have been convinced that there's a God and we serve Him? Bullshit."

Jillian's voice shot up an octave. "How am I supposed to believe you when you won't show me?"

"If you'd agreed to train, I would have shown you. And, sorry, I don't perform on demand. I'm not a circus monkey." *"What would be the point, anyway? When I do show you, you rationalize it away."*

Jillian couldn't help but look at her.

Sam remained focused on the road. "I just said, what would be the point—"

"Yes, yes, okay!" Jillian brought her thumb to her mouth, then dropped it to her lap. She hadn't chewed her nails since she was a teenager.

"Look, normally Fledglings come in willingly. We make contact, they join us, we train them. We don't discuss our gifts with anyone who doesn't belong. You already know more than you should, given that you're refusing to train. If Roberta had her way, you'd be training right now, not sitting in this Jeep with me."

"So turn around and take me back, then!"

"No. Roberta's not a Deiform. I am. I understand that if you don't believe in and accept the gifts, you can't use them." Sam steered the car around a sharp bend in the road. "I also understand where she's coming from. We've never faced this situation before, with a reluctant Fledgling—and an atheist. I suppose she'd hoped that if you learned about the gifts and tried to use them, you'd come around. Since you're refusing to do that, she's hoping that spending time with me will bring you around."

Jillian turned to her. "What do you think?"

"After giving it some thought, I realized that Roberta might be right about taking you with me. Seeing me in action might help." Her eyes flicked to Jillian's face. "You need a reality check."

"*I* need a reality check?" Jillian shrieked. "No freaking comment!"

Sam ignored her outburst. "Ideally, we wouldn't have contacted you until you gave us some indication that you wanted to come in. Jim was told to wait." "Part of it may have been my fault. I was playing the role of a spiritual seeker. I can understand why Jim thought I'd be open to his story."

"Maybe," Sam said tersely. "Whatever the reason, you're here now. I'm going to focus on clearing your name and making sure nobody gets their hands on you. I'll trust the Lord to do the rest."

"And if I decide not to return here with you?"

"That won't happen," Sam stated.

JILLIAN HOPPED OFF the plane and wondered where exactly they'd landed. When she'd asked about their destination, Sam had growled, "Somewhere private," and refused to elaborate. Another plane was parked nearby, and she could make out a house in the distance.

"Is that where we'll be staying?" she asked.

Sam shook her head. "We're staying at a house in town. But I want to hit the ground running, so we're not going there yet." She led Jillian to a gray sedan, popped open the trunk, and tossed her bag inside.

Jillian plunked her bag next to Sam's. "So where are we going?"

Ignoring her, Sam slammed the trunk shut and got into the driver's seat. Perturbed, Jillian climbed in next to her.

"I thought we'd start by—" Sam's phone rang. She pressed it against her ear. "Yeah." Silence, then: "So your hunch was right." Sam snorted. "Really? What a bastard. Which exit?" She listened. "No, we'll find it from there. Yeah, got it. Bye." She hung up.

What is it?"

"I was going to say that we'd start by tracking down the bogus witnesses, but Jeremy just uncovered one of Donaldson's perks."

Jillian clicked her seatbelt into place. "What perk?"

"A house. One he definitely couldn't afford on his salary." Sam started the car. "He'd be more likely to keep any incriminating paperwork or files there, not at his known residence."

"So we'll plant the evidence there?"

Sam nodded. "Let's go check it out." She waved to the pilot and pulled away.

Butterflies took flight in Jillian's stomach. Soon they'd be in the city, where every cop was on the lookout for her. She swallowed. "Is this other residence right in town, or on the outskirts?"

Sam turned onto a rural highway, then glanced at her. "Don't worry. I'll keep you out of the hands of the law." Her forehead creased. "Try not to look so guilty."

"I'm not used to being on the run, okay? I report every penny on my tax return. If I get too much change at a store, I give the excess back. I've never stolen so much as a chocolate bar, even when my friends were pressuring me to do it." She pulled down the visor to reassure herself that her hair hadn't magically reverted to its natural brown. *Damn, no mirror.* She leaned over, tried to catch a glimpse of herself in the side-view mirror. Good, still blonde—and the road behind them was empty. "Nobody's following us."

"I wouldn't expect anybody."

"Wouldn't the, uh, Beguilers be watching the airstrip? You keep saying they'll come after me when I'm off the island."

"They won't be expecting you back so soon. Having said that, it won't take them long to find out you're here. They'll be keeping an eye on our safe houses."

Jillian frowned. "So why don't we stay in a hotel?"

"Because I want to be able to sleep." Sam paused while she passed a slow-moving tractor. "It would be way too easy for them to get into a hotel room."

"If they start to follow us around, they'll stop us from framing Donaldson."

"They'll probably assume you're here because we need you to fake your death. That's the only conceivable reason we'd bring you here so soon, and right into the hornet's nest. If it was me, I'd assume we didn't care about Donaldson. Why would we want to frame him when you're about to die? Why would we care?"

"Revenge?"

"No. We usually wouldn't waste our time on that. In the grand scheme of things, paying him back would mean pulling time and resources away from other matters. But it just so happens that, in this case, we can use him to get what we want, and as I said to Roberta, we can't look the other way this time. He killed a Deiform and a supporter, and framed a Fledgling. I won't lie and say I won't get any pleasure out of making him pay."

Good. She liked that Sam didn't pretend to be a saint. Jillian didn't agree with Sam's views, but at least she wasn't a hypocrite, like most religious types.

"I'm not sure they'd care, even if they figured out what we're up to. The second they find out you're here, their priority will be to capture you, and they know they won't have much time. They'll come up with a plan and execute it. They won't give one whit about Donaldson. He's expendable. Everyone who works for them is."

"So you think they'll come after me, huh?" Should she worry? If not for the fact that someone had done an excellent job of framing her, she'd dismiss the notion that some shadowy Beguilers were out to get her.

"Yes, I do. With luck, we'll be gone before they're ready to move. As Roberta said, the less time you're away from the island, the better."

But I'm not going back!

Sam pulled onto the highway's shoulder and brought the car to a stop. My god, she hadn't heard that, had she? Jillian hadn't spoken the words aloud.

Sam put the car into park and twisted toward Jillian. "I'm not infallible. Your chances of surviving have gone way up because I'm with you. But even though we always have seasoned Deiforms work with green ones for a while, we've lost a couple. And they were trained."

Fear snaked through Jillian, defying her skepticism. "Maybe they'll just tip off the police and let me rot in jail, as they originally intended," she said hopefully.

"No. We're past that point now." Sam's quiet voice frightened Jillian further. "They'll capture you and try to turn you . . . and if that doesn't work, they'll play with you, then kill you." She met Jillian's eyes. "So you listen to me. You must follow one rule. Just one rule. If I say, 'Hang onto me,' do it. Grab me. I don't care who we're with, where we are, or what we're doing. If I say, 'Hang onto me,' do it. No questions, no arguments. Got it?"

"Got it." What harm would grabbing Sam do?

"In fact, let's try it now. If we're wrong about you, I don't want to find out at the worst possible moment. Hang onto me."

Jillian hesitated.

"Hang onto me!"

"Okay." She grabbed Sam's arm. Her surroundings shimmered, then faded away—except for Sam. Jillian could still see her and feel her arm, but Sam appeared ethereal, and Jillian could barely make out where Sam ended and the brilliant light around her began. "Sam!" she called, but heard nothing. She looked down at herself, went to touch her leg with a glimmering hand, and sucked in her breath when her fingers met her jeans and solid flesh. Her stomach lurched. She lifted her head and gazed at the dashboard. The clock hadn't changed. A van raced past on the highway.

Sam put the car into drive. "You can let go now."

Jillian consciously loosened her grip, hoping her fingernails hadn't left a mark. "What happened? What was that?"

"All you need to know is that I'm now one hundred percent sure you're a Fledgling. I was only 99.9 percent sure before." Sam pulled back onto the road. "What's the rule?"

"If you say, 'Hang onto me,' then do it," Jillian repeated dutifully, her mind racing. Had she blacked out for a second? Had Sam somehow . . . what, drugged her? *Get real. What happened?*

She was still asking herself that question when Sam pulled off the highway. "Why are we pulling off here?"

"Because Donaldson apparently didn't want his two homes in the same city. I guess he was afraid someone might spot him."

"Why keep his other home?" she asked, then said, "It's okay. I get it." He needed an address that wouldn't raise eyebrows, especially at work. If the experience back on the highway hadn't left her so unsettled, she would have immediately understood. She'd spent her career uncovering assets people couldn't explain.

"The existence of a second home will bolster the case we're building against him," Sam said. "You good at reading a map?"

"I think I can handle that."

Sam pointed to the glove compartment. "Should be one in there."

"What, no GPS?" Jillian said as she pulled out the map and unfolded it.

"No GPS, nobody tracking us. Sometimes the old-fashioned methods are the best."

After looking for a street sign, Jillian found their location on the map. "Where are we going?" She looked for the address Sam gave her. "It's not far. Take the third left from here, then . . . the second right. That's his street."

"Okay."

Jillian gazed out the window and watched the mansions with their long driveways, three-car garages, and manicured lawns whip past. "He'll be on the right," she said when they turned onto Donaldson's street.

"He might be there."

Jillian turned toward Sam and slid down, as if she were napping.

Sam slowed the car, then stopped. "Nobody in sight. Want to take a peek?"

Still slumped, she rolled to her right and peered out the window. Her blood boiled. That son of a bitch was living it up in a freaking house fit for royalty, while she was being hunted for a double murder. Two restored antique cars sat in the driveway, a fountain—a goddamn fountain!—gurgled away near the oh-so-perfect path leading up to the double front door that would probably be opened by a smiling maid. "You think he got this for killing Jim?"

"No, it looks too lived-in to be a recent reward, but maybe one of those antique cars was just delivered."

"I bet he has an in-ground pool," Jillian muttered. She would have been stuck in a cell smaller than the damn pool and eating prison food for the rest of her life, while he sunned himself next to some bimbo with beach-ball boobs that defied gravity. Mercifully, Sam pulled away and left Donaldson's residence behind before Jillian could smash her fist through the window.

"This is the sort of neighbourhood that calls the cops when riff-raff loiters," Sam said.

A giggle escaped Jillian's lips.

Sam eyed her. "What?"

"If you're what you say you are . . ." Then again, one of them *was* wanted for murder, and Jillian assumed they'd break into Donaldson's at some point.

"We need to know the security and the layout of the house," Sam said.

"You sure you can't read minds?"

Sam glanced at her again.

"Never mind. Can't Jeremy get all that?"

"He couldn't find it, but no matter. We'll come back later, when it's dark."

But they couldn't break in until . . . she'd wait and see. "What next?"

Sam patted her stomach. "I'm getting hungry."

"Yeah, me too."

"Let's go to the safe house. We could grab a bite somewhere around here, but I don't want to risk running into Donaldson, and the less you're out and about, the better."

Jillian cursed her mild apprehension. "You said they'll be watching the safe houses."

"Yeah, they will be." Sam shot her a reassuring look. "They won't make a move today."

Well, that was comforting.

JILLIAN'S SKIN CRAWLED as she climbed out of the sedan, even though Sam had driven into a garage. Was someone outside, watching? Had he seen her hunched down in the passenger seat? Was he already on the phone? She jumped when the trunk popped open. Fortunately, Sam didn't notice her reaction.

Jillian hefted her bag from the trunk and followed Sam into a hallway. She didn't accept that Satan was after her, but those who'd framed her could be. Why kill her, though? If she was a pawn caught between two opposing criminal groups, why wouldn't the Beguilers just tip off the police? Then again, if they believed that she'd joined their rivals and could give them details of the Fellowship's operations—no, they'd still be able to get to her in prison. Maybe they thought the Fellowship would kill her, rather than allow that to happen. Jesus, for all she knew, Sam could be under orders to eliminate her.

Get a grip on yourself! She was seeing bogeymen everywhere. If the Fellowship wanted her dead, they could have killed her on the island and dumped her body in the water. Everything she'd seen, heard, and experienced indicated that they wanted her to join them. She'd go so far as to say that they sincerely believed she was a Fledgling. Their only danger to her was not accepting no for an answer. Once she was in the clear, they'd have to resort to kidnapping and forcible confinement to get her back to that island.

Jillian took a deep, calming breath. Hell, she had to trust *someone*, and right now, that person was Sam, despite their differences when it came to God and everything associated with Him. Sam had supported Jillian's desire to "do it her way," and had said that Jillian must willingly train or there was no point. If she refused, Sam wouldn't like it, but she'd accept it.

Her eyes adjusting to the dim light, Jillian focused on her surroundings. Despite it being late afternoon, all the blinds were drawn on the main floor. Sam flicked on a light. "How many safe houses are there?" Jillian asked as she surveyed the tidy living room. No photos, no knick-knacks, no indication that anybody called this home.

"We have safe houses all over the world," Sam said. "One in every capital, more in many countries."

That must be expensive. Again, she wondered how the Fellowship was funded. How old was it?

Motioning for Jillian to follow her, Sam climbed the stairs to the second floor. "Looks like we're the only ones here," she said, after peering into all the bedrooms. She tossed her bag into the bedroom closest to the top of the stairs. "I usually use this one."

Curious, Jillian peered inside. Nope, no personal touches in here, either. She hadn't seen Sam's room on the island; her perpetually closed door had dissuaded Jillian from intruding. Maybe Sam's bedroom housed her personal possessions, or maybe it was against the rules to own anything except clothes.

Sam moved to the bedroom next to hers. "Why don't you use this one?"

"Sure." Jillian dropped her bag inside the door. Too bad they couldn't go shopping while they were here. "Is there a laundry room?"

Sam nodded. "I'll show you. Let's go to the basement. Security's down there."

While slumped in the passenger seat, Jillian had watched Sam open the garage door by punching a code into what definitely wasn't a run of the mill garage door opener.

Sam paused outside the bedroom across from hers and gazed through the doorway.

"What is it?"

"This is the bedroom Jim usually used."

Jillian glanced inside. Nope, nothing personal.

"While he was waiting for you, he had his own apartment. Since he was going to be out here for a while, meeting people, he needed more of a life than we usually have, in case anyone got nosy." Sam folded her arms. "We had no idea how long it would take for you to show up. All Roberta saw was Jim at the community centre, waiting for you. I wish she'd seen me, instead."

"If she had, you might be dead," Jillian said quietly.

"Maybe, maybe not." She dropped her arms to her sides. "I want to know how they got him. Who was close to him? We have a list of names, but who did he trust? Who did Joanna trust?"

"I don't know. I mainly worked with Mike. Until that night Jim called me, I only ever saw and spoke to him at services and meetings. Others were always around. He didn't seem to favour anyone, including me." She shifted her weight. "I wish I could help."

Sam heaved a sigh. "I shouldn't keep you off the island a minute longer than I have to, but I need to know what happened. I want to check out Jim's apartment. The police have searched it, but they don't know him like I do—did. Something that seemed perfectly normal to them might be a red flag for me. But my instructions are to clear your name and get you back to safety."

"What will a couple of extra hours matter?" No need to point out that Sam could take all the time she wanted, because Jillian's feet weren't leaving the mainland. Not only would it be insensitive to harp on that now, but she felt partially responsible for Jim's death and genuinely wanted to help Sam.

"Thank you," Sam murmured.

"No problem," Jillian said, though she reconsidered her words when Sam's eyes narrowed and she said, "How good of a shot are you?"

Chapter Ten

Hoping that the dark and her slumped position had hidden her from probing eyes, Jillian raised her head and settled back into the sedan's passenger seat. The security room in the basement had impressed her. Multiple cameras observed the exterior of the safe house; one had picked up a man Sam recognized. They were probably being followed, so Jillian wasn't surprised when Sam turned down a road that led away from the highway.

Since Sam didn't seem in the mood to talk, Jillian decided not to strike up a conversation with her. They hadn't chatted much over dinner, either. Sam had spent most of it studying a map Jeremy had sent of the area around Donaldson's house, and had left the table at one point to make a phone call. Jillian hadn't minded. When she wasn't working a case, she usually ate alone. Over the course of the meal, she'd convinced herself that she must have imagined what had happened back on the highway, when she'd hung onto Sam's arm. No more than a few seconds had passed. They hadn't left the car. Sam had appeared . . . ethereal . . . spiritual . . . and so had Jillian's own hand and leg. Maybe something had briefly affected her vision. She'd felt peckish. Low blood sugar? Stress? She'd let Sam's warnings about the Beguilers get to her. God, she hoped it would only take a few days to frame Donaldson. She wanted her life back, the one in which everyone was sane.

Sam's phone rang. "Two streets away," she said to the caller, then hung up.

"What's going on?"

"We're changing cars. We need to lose the blue van. Get ready."

Jillian didn't turn around to look. She released her seatbelt.

Sam turned onto a boulevard with cars parked on both sides. She flashed her high beams. A second later, brakes screeched. Horns blared. When Sam hung a right, Jillian glimpsed a cab that had pulled out into the traffic behind them and blocked the road. Sam pulled over. "Out!" she barked.

Jillian swung the door open and hopped out. Sam grabbed the knapsack she'd thrown into the backseat. "Over here." She ran to an SUV parked in front of the sedan, its engine already running. A woman climbed out of the driver's seat. "Tell Bill he did good," Sam said to the woman. She turned to Jillian. "Get in."

Jillian climbed into the SUV. In a rush to get away, Sam pulled her door shut, plunked the knapsack into Jillian's lap, and floored it. Jillian lurched back into her seat.

"Sorry," Sam said, glancing her way.

"Don't worry about it," Jillian murmured over the SUV's nagging "fasten your seatbelt" beeps. She tossed the knapsack onto the backseat, then snapped her seatbelt into place. This time she couldn't resist twisting to look out the back window. The sedan was directly behind them. When they reached the next intersection, it went left, while they turned right.

"No point making it easy for them," Sam said. At the next red light, she belted herself in. "It's almost eight. Let's listen to the news." She turned on the radio and tuned in to an all-news station.

Jillian tensed. During their drive from Donaldson's to the safe house earlier that day, she'd thought about suggesting that they listen to the radio, but had decided she'd rather not know what, if anything, the media was reporting about her. Now she'd find out. She tried to calm herself as the hourly ditty and requisite commercial played, and relaxed slightly when the lead story was about a fire, not her. But then . . .

"Police are still on the lookout for Jillian Campbell, the accused double murderer who escaped from custody earlier this week. In a press conference this morning, Chief Williams said that detectives are following up on tips and reiterated that Campbell is dangerous and should not be approached. If you have information about Campbell's whereabouts, you should call police or Crime Stoppers."

"Following up on tips?" Jillian blurted.

"From people who've never seen you in their lives," Sam said. "Relax. You're already almost yesterday's news."

Jillian smiled weakly. "Can we listen to a music station, please?"

Sam switched to a local pop station. Jillian half-heartedly tapped her foot along with the song, now grateful that Sam was in a quiet mood. They didn't speak until they were in Donaldson's neighbourhood.

"There should be a park farther down this road," Sam murmured. A minute later, she pulled into its parking lot. "Donaldson's house backs onto this," she said as she dragged her knapsack from the backseat. When Sam moved away from the car, Jillian fell into step with her.

As they left the parking lot, a car parked underneath a tree caught her eye. Darkest spot in the lot, people in the back seat—someone was having a good time. Sam glanced in the car's direction; her expression didn't change. They strolled along a path that would likely be teeming with cyclists, joggers, and walkers at an earlier hour. Jillian's heart pounded when she spotted a man jogging toward them. She lowered her head.

Seconds later, Sam patted her arm. "He's behind us. He didn't even look at you."

Her head still down, she twisted to look at Sam. "No?"

"Nobody really sees anybody these days." Sam nudged her off the path. "Over here." She quickened her pace as they walked across the grass into a wooded area. "Careful, it's starting to slope."

Jillian gingerly navigated through the trees and brush. The trees thinned as they reached a sudden downslope. Near its bottom, she could make out a crooked chain link fence the earth was slowly swallowing. Ah, now she understood. The park stood on high ground. She gazed down into the backyards on Donaldson's street, but couldn't see much in the twilight.

Sam counted houses with her finger. She pointed at one and motioned for Jillian to follow her. Moving parallel to the fence, they crept toward the back of Donaldson's house. A rock rolled down the slope when Jillian almost slipped. "Careful," Sam said over her shoulder. A moment later, she stopped. "I think that's his."

Jillian turned to look. Yep, there were the pool lights. Bastard.

"I'll confirm it's his place before I go in."

"We're going in?"

"No, I'm going in."

"I thought we were still waiting for the forged documents."

"We are. I'd like to know the layout of the house and the security situation before we break in."

Okay, I'm completely lost, Jillian admitted.

Sam crouched and ran her hand over the dirt.

"What are you doing?"

"Looking for a comfortable spot." Sam picked stones out of the dirt and tossed them away. "This'll do. Come closer."

Jillian edged over to her, her breathing sounding unnaturally loud and the gloom suddenly closing in on her. If she screamed, would anyone hear her?

Sam met her eyes. "There comes a time in every growing . . . association, when you have to take a leap of faith and trust the other person. I'm going to do that now." She shrugged the knapsack off her back and handed it to Jillian. "Put this on."

Startled, Jillian didn't argue. She slid her arms through the straps and hoisted the knapsack onto her back.

Sam pointed to a spot near the area she'd cleared. "Okay, sit here and get comfortable."

Jillian sat cross-legged, wondering what would come next. Sam crouched next to her. The top of the knapsack slapped against the back of Jillian's head. "Here." Sam handed Jillian a flashlight. "This will draw attention, so don't use it unless you need to leave in a hurry." Jillian took the flashlight, then frowned when Sam fished the SUV's key from her pocket and held it out to her. "Take it." She plunked it into Jillian's open palm. "Oh, and one last thing." As Jillian slipped the key into her pocket, Sam unzipped her hoodie and drew out a semi-automatic pistol.

Jillian hesitated, then took it from her. "Is it loaded?"

"Yes," Sam said, sounding surprised.

Jillian looked down at the pistol in her hand and swallowed. She was trained to use this type of firearm, but she'd never shot anybody.

"We're doing this tonight because the Beguilers won't be ready to strike this early. If you sit quietly, nobody else will know you're here, either." Jillian felt embarrassed when Sam peered at her and added, "You'll be fine. I'm probably being overly cautious, but I'll feel a lot better knowing that you can defend yourself and get away."

"Let me go with you."

"You can't." Sam crouched in front of her. "Now, there's a phone in the knapsack. If you have to leave, just turn it on when you can and we'll find you. You can also reach us by calling any of the numbers in the contact list. I'd suggest finding somewhere to sit tight and wait, rather than driving around. So, you ready?"

Not really. "Yeah," Jillian said, clutching the flashlight in her left hand and the pistol in her right.

Sam nodded. "I'm going to lie down and not really be here for a while. Don't be afraid to leave me, if you have to. I'll be okay. Worry about yourself."

"What do you mean, you won't really be here?" Jillian asked.

"What I said." Sam stretched out her legs and slowly lay back. Her head touched the ground an inch from Jillian's crossed legs. She grimaced and sat up, brushed a couple of twigs away, and lowered herself to a supine position again.

Jillian leaned over Sam and stared at her. "What are you doing?"

"I'll try not to be long." Sam crossed her arms across her chest and closed her eyes. Her face slackened; she paled, her body relaxed, then . . . a perceptible stillness.

Jillian's breath caught in her throat. "Sam?" she hissed. "Sam!"

Nothing.

Trying not to panic, she stood the flashlight on the ground and knelt. "Sam?" *Damn it! And screw this!* Knowing that menacingly waving the gun around would be as far as she could go if pressed, Jillian set it next to the flashlight, bent over Sam, and poised her ear a couple of inches from Sam's nose and mouth. She listened. Her shoulders slumped with relief. Sam was breathing, albeit slowly; Jillian could only see Sam's chest rise and fall when she concentrated on looking for the motion. She leaned back on her heels. Should she slap Sam and see what happened? Because, right now, that was what she freaking felt like doing! *What is this?* Was Sam in some type of meditative state? Was it a show? All Jillian could do was wait.

With a sigh, she sat cross-legged again and watched Sam's face. *You do realize that, if I'm caught now, sitting with a gun next to someone who at first glance appears dead, I'm toast, right?* No answer.

God, she was going insane. She needed to get away from these people. Well, she had the key to the SUV. She had fake ID in her back pocket. Okay, no money, but she had a phone. She could call Mom and Danny and arrange to meet them somewhere. And then what? Wait for Sam and the Fellowship to find her? Because she knew, in the pit of her stomach, that they would. Whatever they were, whoever they worked for, they were powerful and had everything they needed at their fingertips. Cars, houses, guns, technology—she doubted she'd last more than twenty-four hours before they caught up with her. Maybe she should check herself for an implanted tracking chip.

Would they let her walk after they'd cleared her name? Sam would. Roberta was a different matter, but Jillian trusted Sam. In fact, if she was honest with herself, Sam was the main reason she was sitting here, rather than making a run for it. Even if she thought she could get away and hide from them, she wouldn't willingly leave Sam alone and vulnerable in the park—and she wouldn't want to betray her trust. She also wanted her name cleared. If she were to run away, Roberta could decide to forget about that and drag her back to the island. But, right now, Jillian was staying here for Sam; she was too responsible for her own good. *I get the feeling you are, too,* she thought at Sam. No answer. *You'd better have a good explanation for this.* Okay, if she started talking to Sam out loud, she'd know she'd truly lost it.

The sun had fully set; the light breeze had a nip to it. Jillian unfolded her legs and hugged them to her chest. How many minutes had passed? Ten? Fifteen? Sam had said she wouldn't be long. Jillian could still see Sam's pale face; it was never truly dark in a city. Wait. Was the chill colouring Sam's cheeks, or . . .

Sam's eyelids fluttered, then her eyes opened. She stared at Jillian; her mouth turned up at the corners. "I knew you'd still be here."

Why, of all the arrogant—how dare she— Jillian wanted to slap her again.

Sam sat up. "No, don't," she snapped when Jillian started to stand. "Give me the knapsack."

Jillian shrugged it off her back. Sam opened it and pulled out a notebook and pen. "I want to get this down before I forget. Can you hold the flashlight?" she asked as she opened the notebook and poised the pen over an empty page.

Jillian turned on the flashlight and illuminated the page. "What did you—"

"Shh! Let me get this down." She drew a rectangle, then a square within the rectangle, and labelled it *Living Room*. Next, the dining room. The stairs with an arrow pointing up. A recreation room.

Shocked, Jillian watched her complete the main floor, then flip to a new page and start the second floor.

"There's a safe behind this panel," Sam murmured, making a note along the master bedroom wall. When she added a study, she sketched in a desk. "Another good place to leave a surprise package. Oh, and the security system is nothing special. Jeremy and Emma will know how to disarm it." Sam quickly drew the basement, then clipped the pen to the notebook and closed it. "Too bad we can't go in tonight. Apart from some woman watching a movie in the rec room, there's nobody else there."

"She's probably the maid."

Sam slowly shook her head. "I don't think so. I doubt the maid would be lounging around in silk lingerie, drinking wine. There are photos of her around the house, too. She's not his wife."

So the bastard had a mistress tucked away in his hideaway? Why wasn't she surprised? Okay, hang on, here. Was she supposed to believe that Sam had somehow floated down to the house and through an open window? How did Sam know all this?

"Might as well keep the flashlight on." Sam's brow furrowed. "Where's the gun?"

Jillian lifted it from the ground and sheepishly handed it to her. "I know how to use one, but . . . And I didn't want to accidentally shoot you."

Sam's mouth twitched. "Good to know." After holstering the gun, she buckled the knapsack closed and hoisted it onto her back. "Let's go."

The flashlight's beam guided them as they retraced their path back to the SUV. Bursting with questions, Jillian handed Sam the key, and finally gave into her curiosity as they pulled out of the parking lot.

"So what am I supposed to believe?" she blurted. "That you somehow divined the layout of the house?"

Sam kept her eyes on the road. "No, I went inside."

"What, you went in spiritual form or something?"

Sam nodded. "Some refer to it as astral projection."

"Is that one of the gifts?"

"Yes."

"So when we get around to planting the evidence, we'll have to enter the house in physical form because you can't carry anything when you're in spiritual form. Correct?"

"Yes."

Uh-huh. Jillian jiggled her leg as she considered Sam's far-fetched, but predictable, response. First, the layout Sam had drawn could be bogus. Jillian wouldn't know until they entered the house. Second, she only had Sam's word for it that Jeremy couldn't obtain the house's floor plan. Sam could have used a drug to put herself into a trancelike state, then regurgitated the plan she'd studied, not the plan she'd memorized as she'd toured through Donaldson's house as a ghost. As for the safe, desk, and other details Sam had included . . . maybe the Fellowship had photos of the house's interior. Maybe Sam hoped Jillian wouldn't focus on comparing the actual layout to the sketched one when they broke in. Plus, furniture could be moved. Nope, Jillian wasn't buying it.

When they stopped at a red light. Sam turned to her. "Let me ask you something. Out of all the people we could recruit, why would we choose you? Why be so persistent about you? Don't you think we'd want people who are interested in joining us? Who don't need to be convinced? That's how it usually goes."

Jillian folded her arms. "I don't know, Sam, you tell me."

"Because we don't get to choose. He does."

"No, Roberta does. Roberta chooses."

Sam glanced at her. "Roberta's right about you."

"How do you know?" Jillian snapped.

"I know, because . . ." *I can talk to you like this.* "And earlier today, I confirmed the gifts are within you." When Jillian remained silent, Sam said, "I won't force you to train. As I've said to you and Roberta, that won't work. But you can't have your old life back. That life is dead. If you want to live, your only choice is to be reborn as one of us."

"I don't believe that." The voice she sometimes heard in her head? It wasn't coming from Sam. Her own brain must be filling in the blanks, or Sam was using some voice-throwing technique to confuse her. By gifts, Sam could mean tricks and sleight of hand. Jillian had no intention of relenting and joining the cult to find out. "I believe that you believe it, but I don't believe it."

"You will. If you don't, you'll die."

"Why? If I refuse to go back to the island, will you kill me?" Forget about the shadowy Beguilers. She only had the Fellowship's word for it that they existed and were out to get her. That trouble on the way to the park could have been a show. After all, for some unknown reason, Sam's group desperately wanted to recruit her. Their powerful adversaries could be a fabrication meant to frighten Jillian into accepting the Fellowship as her only salvation.

The light turned green. Sam stepped on the accelerator. "No, I won't kill you." She was silent for a moment. "I almost wish it would be me. I'd be merciful," she said softly.

Jillian swallowed. "Nobody's going to kill me." *Are you sure? They killed Jim and Joanna.* Not Sam's voice. Her own.

Chapter Eleven

JILLIAN DROPPED HER spoon into her empty cereal bowl and gazed across the kitchen table at Sam, who'd already finished her breakfast and was reading something on her phone. "I've been thinking about last night."

Sam lifted her head and waited.

"You gave me a gun. We're going to break into Donaldson's house. We're falsifying evidence."

"You saw the evidence they have against you. We have to explain that evidence away. We're not setting up anyone who's innocent, unlike what they did to you."

She could appreciate that, but . . . "I'm trying to get a sense of your moral compass. You say you serve God . . ."

Sam snorted. "So, what? I should be out there chasing criminals, or busting kids for shoplifting? Or maybe I should be making people's dreams come true, swooping in and dropping money bags at their feet just as their houses are about to be foreclosed. Or maybe you think I should be showing some poor, lost soul what his true purpose is in life. Or reuniting long-lost relatives." She shook her head. "You've watched too many angel shows on TV. That's not what we do. I don't flit around sprinkling fairy dust."

Jillian pointed at herself. "Do you think I'm the sort of person who watches angel shows? I figure there are more important things to do than make people's dreams come true. If there is a God, I'm sure He doesn't give a crap about who wins the World Series. I get that. But guns? Breaking and entering?"

"I obey God's law, not man's law. Most of the time, they—" Sam searched for an appropriate word "—intersect. But if a man-made law is holding me back from getting something done that serves the greater good, tough."

Jillian lifted a brow. "The end justifies the means?"

Sam thumped her fist on the table. "I operate at a different level than everyone else. I move in a world most people don't know exists, in which man's law doesn't mean a thing." She raised a finger. "I would never harm an innocent, in any way. But if I need to pick a lock to carry out the Lord's work, I will. I don't expect you to understand, nor do I need your approval. If you believe the letter of the law should be obeyed no matter what . . ." Sam slid the phone across the table. "Call the cops and arrange to turn yourself in. I'm itching to get back to the island, anyway."

They glared at each other, Jillian refusing to acknowledge the phone under her nose. Her situation was different, as Sam freaking-well knew! *Is it? How?* When the phone rang, she jumped, then pushed it back to Sam, who picked it up.

"Yeah." Sam listened. "No kidding. Can you prove it was Donaldson?" She paused. "Too bad. But you can lay a paper trail from there? Great, that simplifies things for us. Good work." Her eyes flicked to Jillian. "We're fine. Talk to you later." She hung up. "Jeremy and Emma found out why those witnesses fingered you. One witness now has much richer parents, and the other one won't have the law after him for ducking child support payments. The mother of his kids apparently hit the jackpot."

Jillian seethed. Two low-lifes had decided to let her rot in prison in return for money. She was a human being! How much had her life been worth to them? A couple thousand dollars? Ten thousand?

"They can handle it from the island, so there's no need for us to let ourselves into the witnesses' humble abodes," Sam said.

"What's left?"

"Planting evidence at Donaldson's place. We also have to figure out how we're going to pull the trigger." Sam scratched her head. "Roberta called me last night with an idea. Before I agree to it, I want to think about it a bit more."

"What is it?"

Sam pushed away from the table. "If I agree to it, I'll tell you. Let's go to Jim's."

After placing her dirty dishes into the sink, Jillian followed Sam to the garage. A minute later, they were on the road. Sam glanced in the rearview mirror. "Nobody," she murmured. "Which is worrisome. They've already come up with a plan."

"It's good that nobody's on our tail. I doubt the switching cars stunt would fool them again," Jillian said, trying to see a bright side.

"I don't care if they know we're at Jim's place. It would be odd if none of us checked it out. I don't really care if they know that we're interested in Donaldson, either." Sam slowed down to turn a corner. "As I said, they don't watch out for their people. They're all expendable."

Speaking of people . . . "Who helped us last night?"

"We have supporters scattered across the continent who are still in the system."

"Not dead, you mean?"

Sam nodded. "Bill, the guy who drove the cab last night, lives here in town. Shauna, the one at the SUV, flew in a couple of days ago, to take care of Jim. She's on record as Jim's next of kin."

Jillian frowned. "What about Joanna?"

"She was still in the system."

"Oh."

"Shauna won't touch Jim's apartment until we tell her we're finished with it." Sam glanced at Jillian. "I have a key, so don't worry. We won't be breaking in."

Jillian's face tightened. "What about Joanna's place?"

"Her family will be all over it by now." Sam paused. "Jim should have stayed at the safe house. He could still have had an apartment for show."

"They didn't kill him at his apartment, right? So whatever happened, they lured him somewhere. I don't see how staying at the safe house would have made a difference."

"Maybe you're right." Sam gripped the steering wheel. "I wish you'd stayed on the island. I'll do my best to protect you, but—"

"I wanted to leave the island," Jillian said firmly. "If something happens to me, it won't be your fault." Jillian wasn't surprised that the tension in Sam's face didn't ease. If she were in Sam's shoes, she'd blame herself, too. God, she hated that they were cut from the same cloth.

They drove the rest of the way in silence. Sam slowed down on a downtown street not far from the community centre and pointed to an apartment complex. "That's it." She frowned. "See anywhere to park? Jim didn't have a spot in the garage."

Jillian peered out at the cars parked bumper to bumper. "No. Bad time of day."

Sam circled the block, with no luck. "I'll try the next block."

Jillian's stomach churned. The less distance they had to walk, the better. Wandering around a park at night wasn't the same as walking downtown. People were everywhere. She could bump into someone she knew. "Maybe you should have left me at the safe house."

"No. The safest place for you to be is with me. Oh, look, someone's leaving." She flicked on the indicator and waited for them to pull out, then quickly claimed the spot.

"Is there a hat in there?" Jillian asked when Sam lifted the ubiquitous knapsack from the trunk.

"Someone left this behind." She held out a crumpled baseball cap.

Figured. Jillian usually avoided hats that made her look like a dork, but she'd make an exception this time.

"Looks like it might rain," Sam said.

Jillian looked up and nodded. She pulled the baseball cap onto her head and fell into step with Sam. "What will you look for at Jim's place?"

"I don't know. It's one of those 'I'll know it when I see it' sort of situations. I might not find anything."

They turned a corner. Jillian tensed. A police cruiser sat at the light. She locked eyes with the cop in the passenger seat. When he straightened, she ducked her head. "Sam!"

"I saw." Sam gripped her arm. "Don't run." She glanced over her shoulder. "Shit."

Jillian's heart leaped into her mouth. "What?"

"They're getting out of the car."

Adrenaline coursed through her. If not for Sam's restraining hand, she'd bolt.

"Down here." Sam ducked into a laneway running between two apartment buildings, and steered Jillian toward a dumpster standing near one of the building's rear doors. Hell, Jillian was so frightened that if Sam told her to dive in and hide, she'd do it in a heartbeat! But Sam pulled her to the far side of the dumpster, where they couldn't be seen from the street.

Trembling, Jillian pressed against the dumpster's cold steel. "I think I glimpsed them coming into the laneway. They're probably calling for backup. We'll be trapped."

"No, we won't." Sam's grip on Jillian's arm tightened. "Trust me."

Suddenly they were in that other world, with ethereal bodies, silence, light. But Jillian could still feel Sam's hand, just as she'd felt her own leg in the car. She touched her face—and felt flesh. Beams of light raced past as she turned her head toward Sam, reached out . . . A drop of water hit her shoulder. She looked up, into rain. Sam let go of her arm, stepped farther into the laneway, and glanced around. "Let's walk to the other end."

Bewildered, Jillian mutely followed her. When had it started to rain? When they'd hidden next to the dumpster, the pavement had been bone dry and black clouds had hung in the sky. Now it was pouring. The cement was slick, and the patches of grass and dirt behind one of the apartments appeared soaked, but the drop that had hit her shoulder was the first drop she'd felt. Her clothes should be sopping wet.

"Let's pick up the pace," Sam said, breaking into a jog. "Given the weather, nobody will be suspicious."

Anxious to get inside, Jillian put her questions aside and focused on keeping pace with Sam. When they came out of the laneway, an exterior digital clock on a corner store caught her eye. It read *1:13*. *What?* They'd left the safe house at 9:30. *Not possible!*

They continued jogging until they bounded up the cement stairs to Jim's building. In the lobby, Sam fished a key ring from her pocket and collected the mail from Jim's box, then unlocked the security door. An elevator door dinged open. Sam punched the button for the fourth floor and, once there, led Jillian to apartment 415.

Inside, Jillian sank into the first chair she saw and held her head in her hands.

"You all right?" Sam asked.

Her world was coming apart. She needed to make sense of it. "I'll be okay."

Sam crouched in front of her. "I would have thought you'd be used to hiding in plain sight, so to speak." She sounded concerned, not critical.

"This is different. Usually I'm the good guy." Jillian let go of her head and met Sam's eyes. "Are you going to tell me how it's after one in the afternoon?"

Sam pushed herself up. "I'll tell you later, okay?"

She blew out an exasperated sigh. "I need to know!"

"And I'll tell you. Over dinner, I promise. Right now, I want to look around."

"Fine. I guess we won't be having lunch, since we only ate breakfast half an hour ago." Sam's answering silence didn't help Jillian's mood. She hated being in the dark, especially with so much at stake.

"Think you can help look around?" Sam said.

Jillian nodded, eager to focus on something else.

"Look for anything with names, meeting times, uh . . . anything that might suggest that someone had contact with Jim outside the services." Sam surveyed the room. "He should have a computer." She wandered down the narrow hallway, then returned. "Okay, I'll start in his office. Why don't you take the bedroom? I don't see anything in the living room. No messages on the phone . . ." She read the two envelopes she still held and snorted. "Junk mail. The guy exists for a few months and he's already on lists." She dropped them onto an end table. "Come on."

Sam pointed at the first room off the hallway as she passed it. Jillian peered inside, then walked into the bedroom. Unlike the rooms at the safe house, this one looked occupied. Framed photos of nature scenes adorned the walls. A pair of pants was draped over a chair. The double bed was neatly made. If the Beguilers *had* taken Jim's bed sheet and put it on her bed, they wouldn't have left his bed in an untidy state. She lifted one of the pillows, drew down the blanket and flat sheet, and wasn't surprised to see a blue fitted sheet.

A notebook and pen sat on the nightstand next to the bed. The police must have leafed through it already, but Jillian picked it up and skimmed its pages. Apparently Jim had jotted down ideas when he was in bed, perhaps when a problem kept him awake. She'd read that writing down whatever weighed on one's mind made it easier to fall back to sleep, but she'd never tried it. Waking in the middle of the night was never a problem for her. Life had always been uneventful, routine.

She closed the notebook and set it where she'd found it. Feeling like an intruder, she slid open the nightstand drawer. A couple of pencils rolled around next to a Bible. She hesitated, then lifted the Bible from the drawer and opened it. *New International Version.* A piece of notepaper was visible behind the thin title page. She slid it from the Bible and read two scribbled lines.

Matthew 18:6-7
Ephesians 1:7

Curious, and wondering if she'd find more notes within the Bible, she leafed through its pages. A wave of melancholy tightened her throat. She couldn't help but think about Dad, and how a book that had enthralled her had lost its magic. Even now, she felt compelled to read her favourite verses. The Bible itself wasn't the problem; she'd be the first to concede that it contained timeless parables and nuggets of wisdom. It was everything associated with it—the pulpit, the pews, the judgemental attitude, the hypocrisy, the hate. But sometimes she asked herself if she'd gone too far, discarded the wheat along with the chaff.

She couldn't deny that when she'd believed, she'd felt happier and more fulfilled. Losing her belief in God had left a void that muted every aspect of her life. She wished she could recapture the magic, go back to the time when she never questioned, rarely doubted, accepted that she was God's daughter, that He cared about her, and that, in the end, wrongs would be righted and justice would be served. It was better than a crap world in which the good guys often finished last, nobody gave a shit, and, in the end, none of it mattered anyway.

What was the point? Why was she so hell-bent on clearing her name when she'd cease to exist? In a hundred years, just about everybody on the planet would be dead, and life would steamroll on as if they'd never existed. Some might be remembered through history, but most would be forgotten. The drama, the tears, the joys, the stress, the accomplishments, the pain, the growth as a person—pointless. All for absolutely nothing. So why bother? Why care? Because the human race progressed? Really? There was still war, still murder, still greed, still hate, still people bitching about trivial problems and coveting the latest gadget, while many in the world didn't have enough food to eat. So why give a shit?

With a sigh, she continued to turn the pages. A business card was tucked in the Book of Malachi. She pulled it out and peered at it. *Ellen Marsh, MBA.* Was it the same Ellen who'd sometimes attended a service? Sam wanted names. Jillian tossed the card onto the nightstand and searched for more clues. A short bookmark had slipped down into Matthew. Jim must have had 18:6-7 on his mind.

If anyone causes one of these little ones—those who believe in me—to stumble, it would be better for them to have a large millstone hung around their neck and to be drowned in the depths of the sea. Woe to the world because of the things that cause people to stumble! Such things must come, but woe to the person through whom they come!

Had someone raised Jim's suspicions? Jillian turned the pages faster, hoping to find more. She slowed down at Ephesians and found 1:7.

In him we have redemption through his blood, the forgiveness of sins, in accordance with the riches of God's grace . . .

If there was a connection to the Matthew verse, or a message, they eluded Jillian, but she could feel and see a piece of cardboard through the thin page. She flipped it—and couldn't breathe. Her world tipped on its axis. *What the hell is going on?* She sank onto the bed and lifted the photograph the page had obscured. A girl in overalls, a t-shirt, and runners was riding a brand new bike. Jillian turned the photo over. Nothing was written on its back. No matter. She didn't need anyone to identify the twelve-year-old in the photo. *Me.*

Think. Think! They'd claimed they didn't know the identity of the Fledgling, that Jim was told to go out into the world and wait. Bullshit. Who were these people? Why did Jim have a photo of her, taken a few months after Dad died? She remembered that day—her birthday. Mom had tried, really tried, to make it a happy day. Her mask had eventually slipped, but they'd managed a couple of hours of forced gaiety, unaware that someone was watching and taking photographs.

Mom's effort to put her emotional turmoil aside hadn't stretched to using a camera. The family photo albums from when Dad was alive were bursting with photos. After he died . . . one album held all the photos from the years that followed. Who wanted to capture grief, bewilderment, and bitterness for posterity? Not them, but someone else had stood in the shadows and snapped away. One of Jillian's few sunny memories from the gloom following Dad's death—violated.

The Fellowship had lied, but she was trapped. Until they cleared her name, she had nowhere to go but prison. Were they playing her? Would they frame Donaldson, or were they just wearing her down? What about Sam? Tears sprang to her eyes. Horrified, she blinked them back. She'd wanted to trust *someone*. She'd wanted to believe that Sam was on her side, understood her need to clear her name, and supported her desire to exercise her free will and decline to join the Fellowship. Was every word out of Sam's mouth a lie?

Her options were limited. She could throw the Bible aside and make a run for it, but she doubted she'd get very far. If the police didn't get her, Sam would. Jillian had seen enough to know that the Fellowship was powerful. Hiding from them would be impossible. Nope, her original game plan still held. She'd go along and see how it played out—with one condition. She must not go back to the island. If Sam suggested that they return before they'd cleared her name, maybe under the pretense of needing to meet in person with the others, or some other excuse, Jillian would have to run. She'd rather go to prison than be indoctrinated into a cult that was engaging in criminal activity.

She examined the photo again. Good, her hand was steady. She slipped the photo into her back pocket, then flipped through the rest of the Bible and found nothing more. After rifling through Jim's bureau and searching the rest of the bedroom—including under the bed and between the mattresses—she picked up the business card, took a deep breath, and willed herself to walk into Jim's office.

Seated at the computer, Sam looked over her shoulder. She wasn't psychic—the hallway floor creaked. "From his email, it looks like he was counselling a few people. They're all on the list of names we have, so no strangers to investigate. But one woman seemed to need a lot more help recently. She sounded desperate. I could see Jim rushing out to deal with a crisis."

"What's her name?"

Sam looked down at the notepad at her elbow. "Ellen Marsh."

"Ellen Marsh, MBA." When Sam threw her a questioning look, Jillian handed her the business card. "I found it in his Bible."

"Sounds like we need to check out Ellen Marsh." Sam pulled out her phone. "Can you send me everything you have on Ellen Marsh?" she said a moment later, probably to Jeremy. "She's on Jim's list. Thanks." She looked at Jillian. "Did you find anything else?"

"No." She paused. "Why do you think Jim called me, rather than just breaking into my apartment and confronting me? He wanted to come over, said he could prove that what he was saying was true. You don't seem to have any compunction about breaking and entering, so why didn't he just let himself in while I was out?"

"He wasn't to tell you about us until you had an inkling of what you are. You said he thought you ran into a Beguiler, right?"

She nodded.

"He was worried about you, but he probably felt conflicted about contacting you, so he called to get your permission to see you. Or maybe he didn't want to scare you. I don't know." Sam heaved her shoulders, then rolled back the chair. "I'm finished with this room."

"Didn't Jeremy already have everything on Jim's computer?"

"His priority is Donaldson." Sam glanced around. "I already checked his desk. Let's take a quick look around the kitchen and bathroom. I doubt we'll find anything, but you never know."

By the time they'd finished searching the rest of the apartment and coming up empty, Jeremy had sent the file on Ellen Marsh. While Sam skimmed the information on her phone, Jillian gazed out the living room window and noticed that it had stopped raining.

"The police spoke to her, but as someone who knew him, not as a potential accessory to his murder," Sam said. "Let's swing by her place. Hopefully she won't be home."

Jillian turned to her. "Why don't you get the car and call Jim's phone when you're outside? I don't want to be seen again."

Sam frowned. "No, come with me."

"Why, do you think I'll take off?" Jillian snapped.

"No. I don't want to leave you alone and vulnerable."

"Come on, Sam, I'll be all right in here for ten minutes."

Sam shifted her weight. "You'll be safe from the police, and I guess I'm more worried about them right now. The Beguilers didn't follow us here, so they're planning to take you out somewhere else."

"Is that supposed to make me feel better?"

Sam didn't crack a smile. "I'll get the car. I'll call when I'm outside." She gave Jillian the apartment keys. "Lock the door on your way out."

After Sam left, Jillian sat on the sofa and pulled out the photo again. Maybe she *should* take off; she might not get another chance like this. But she had two compelling reasons to stay with the group for now: to clear her name, and to find out why Jim had this photo. Had Jim, or someone else, stalked her all her life? She couldn't tell who the good guys were anymore.

Chapter Twelve

JILLIAN SIPPED COKE up a straw and peered out the window as Sam cruised by Ellen Marsh's house. No signs of life, but that didn't mean the house was empty. They passed several more cookie-cutter houses and turned the corner. With the majority of Marsh's bedroom community away at work or school, the streets were deserted. Parking spots abounded.

Sam pulled over and turned off the engine. "Let me make sure the house is empty. I won't be long." She leaned back in the car seat. Her face slackened.

Jillian shook her head and fought the urge to shout into Sam's ear. Doing so would only attract the attention of any curtain twitchers on the block. She pulled the baseball cap down over her eyes. Hat hair would be the understatement of the year when she finally took it off. Maybe she'd remove it in the bathroom, where she could assess the damage and jump into the shower, if need be. She blew out a sigh and waited for Sam to end her charade.

"Okay," Sam said a few minutes later. "Two German shepherds are home, but they won't be a problem." She paused. "I have reason to believe that Ms. Marsh is on a cruise and won't be back anytime soon. Let's drive around the block and park in front of her house. The less we try to hide, the better." She fired up the engine and pulled away. "You okay?"

"Yeah."

Sam glanced at her. "You've been quiet since Jim's."

Jillian tensed, then consciously relaxed. "I haven't had much to say, that's all. You still owe me an explanation," she said, hoping to distract Sam.

"I promised I'll tell you over dinner, and I will."

When they reached Marsh's house, Sam opened the trunk, pulled two books from a trunk organizer, and held one out to Jillian.

She stared at the Bible. "You have got to be kidding me."

Sam swung her knapsack onto her back and slammed the trunk shut. "You'd be surprised what you can get away with by carrying a Bible and looking . . . serene." She started up Marsh's path.

Jillian hurried after her. "Isn't this taking the Lord's name in vain, or something like that?"

"Not for me. If anyone wants to talk to me about God, I'm up for it." Sam's eyes narrowed. "And not for you, either. You can't take someone's name in vain when you don't believe they exist. Plus, it's not our fault if someone thinks we want to proselytize the neighbourhood." She rang the doorbell, provoking a cacophony of muffled barking.

Okay, so there were dogs. Sam could have found out about them from Jeremy.

"Let's go around the back."

Feeling as if every eye on the street was on her, Jillian tramped across the grass and around the house.

"Love these high privacy fences." Sam shrugged off her knapsack, opened it, and dropped her Bible inside. She drew out a leather case. "Shouldn't take me long," she said, unzipping the case to reveal what Jillian assumed to be a set of lock picks.

Great. If the cops picked her up, could she still claim that she'd never committed a crime? Sam crouched in front of the lock and inserted a pick with a bend at its end. Then she inserted another pick. Jillian swallowed, and turned away while Sam picked the lock. Expecting to hear a siren any minute, she wiped sweat off her brow. Unlike Sam, she wasn't cut out for this. Who was Sam, really? How many houses had she invaded? How many people had she killed?

Sam grunted. "We're in." She quickly slid the picks into the case and threw it into the knapsack, then opened the door and crept inside, motioning for Jillian to follow her. They stepped into the kitchen—

Two barking German shepherds charged toward them. Jillian gasped and froze—then gaped when the barking cut off and the dogs dropped to their stomachs, their wagging tails thumping against the floor. Sam clucked her tongue at them and walked to the fridge. "You see this?"

Still not trusting the dogs, Jillian carefully walked to Sam's side and read the page stuck to the fridge door with a magnet. The email exchange with a friend included instructions for feeding and walking the dogs. She relaxed slightly. The friend wouldn't be by until after work.

"She just happens to suddenly go on a cruise." Sam shook her head. "A cruise for two lives. Though I suppose we might uncover more rewards." She sounded disheartened. "Let's take a quick look around, see if we can find anything else."

"What do you think happened?" Jillian asked as they poked around the living room. "Okay, she was seeing Jim outside the services, but—do you think she killed them?"

"No. I think she lured Jim and Joanna somewhere. She probably didn't know why. The Beguilers could have told her anything about why they wanted to see them at that particular location." Sam flipped through an address book that sat next to the phone. "Jim would have had to have been incapacitated or distracted for them to take him. Maybe Marsh drugged them."

"Why would she agree to do that? Wouldn't she find it suspicious?"

"People see what they want to see and hear what they want to hear. The converse is also true. The Beguilers could have given her a bottle of his favourite wine and told her to share a glass with them." Sam's brow furrowed. "Actually, something like that makes sense. Marsh would be out, too. When she wakes up, Jim and Joanna are gone, leaving a note behind. But it's all speculation. We'll never know what actually happened." She headed for the stairs to the second floor.

Jillian trailed after her. "When Jim and Joanna were found dead, wouldn't Marsh have wondered?"

"If they were found at another location, why would it occur to her that she had something to do with it?" Sam went into the master bedroom. "I never liked the idea of Jim staying out here for so long. When I'm in the world, I'm ultra-careful with people. I'm careful about what I eat and drink. I only meet with someone in private if it's absolutely necessary. I don't have friends. The only place I let my guard down is on the island."

"It must get lonely."

"I'm too busy to be lonely."

Funny, Jillian always told herself the same thing.

After finding nothing in the bedroom, they moved on to a home office. Sam picked up the pad next to the phone and flipped back through its pages. She stopped.

"What is it?"

"J and J, 9, Tony's. Who's Tony?"

"Could be a bar, or a restaurant," Jillian suggested. "Maybe she—or they—slipped them that date-rape drug."

"Maybe." Sam set the pad back exactly how she'd found it. "What time did he phone you?"

"Around 7:30. And I called Donaldson before 8:00."

"If this was an appointment for the same night, they didn't waste any time. Jim might have figured it was okay to leave you while government agents were at your apartment. But again, we just don't know." She glanced at a folded newspaper and snorted. "Marsh circled Jim's obituary. I guess a cruise was more important than going to his funeral."

"Roberta said Jim's remains wouldn't be brought back to the island. If his next of kin on record belongs to the Fellowship, why not?"

"The island's not hidden, but we wouldn't want to lead the police, or anyone else, to it."

"When's the funeral?"

"Tomorrow."

"Are you going?" Jillian asked.

"No. You can't go, and I can't leave you alone."

Still holding the Bible, Jillian folded her arms. "I'm sure I'd be okay at the safe house."

"We held a service for them on the island," Sam said tersely. "Let's finish up here and get out."

Five minutes later, they walked back through the kitchen. The dogs hadn't budged. Sam waved good-bye to them and, once outside, took the time to pick the lock again, this time to lock it. Bibles in hand, they walked to the car.

"Are we going to figure out who, or what, Tony is?" Jillian asked on the way back to the safe house.

"No, I just wanted to confirm that someone Jim trusted probably lured him to his death. He couldn't defend Joanna—or himself." Her lips compressed into a thin line.

Jillian sensed that Sam wasn't in the mood for more conversation, which suited her just fine. She had her own puzzles to work out.

JILLIAN HAD RESISTED the urge to press Sam about their missing hours the moment they sat down to eat, but now they were halfway through their chicken dinner and Sam hadn't raised the subject. Had Sam somehow drugged her earlier that day? And then what? Thrown Jillian over her shoulder and staggered into the apartment building with two cops hot on her heels? Had she blacked out? No, that also wouldn't explain how they'd eluded their pursuers.

What about the dogs? If Sam had known about them in advance, had she stuffed her pockets with treats? No, apart from when Sam had gone to fetch the car, they'd stayed together. Maybe Sam was somehow drugging her on an ongoing basis, with a psychotic drug that distorted reality. Maybe everything that had happened to her since leaving Mom's for the mall was an illusion. And maybe she was Mary freaking Poppins. She let out a louder sigh than she'd intended.

Sam swallowed a mouthful of food. "It's called time shifting."

Jillian put down her knife and fork, and waited for more.

"I can step outside time and re-enter it later on. So can you, but since you're untrained, you can't do it at will, and when you're outside time, everything's distorted for you."

Hang onto me. That's the rule. "But if we're touching, you can take me outside time with you?"

Sam nodded. "It's how I know for sure you're a Fledgling. If you weren't, you couldn't come with me. There are other ways to tell whether someone's a Fledgling, but the ability to time shift is the clincher for me."

"That's what you tested in the car."

Sam nodded.

"But no time passed in the car, according to the clock." Then again . . . "It felt like no time had passed today, either, but somehow

I lost over three hours."

"I can time shift up to a day. I can only shift forward, not backward." Sam's mouth turned up at the corners. "Imagine the havoc we could cause if we could go back in time. God, in His wisdom, doesn't allow that."

Jillian tried to wrap her head around Sam's claim. "So you're saying that we stepped out of time, and then we stepped back into time later, after the police had searched for us and gone."

"Yes."

"How did you know when they'd gone? And what would someone have seen if they were looking out their apartment window?"

"When we stepped out of time? To them, it would have looked as if we'd winked out of existence. As for knowing when to step back in, I can see what's happening in the physical location at which I time shifted. It all whips by at top speed, as if I'm watching a movie on fast forward." Sam mimed pressing a button on a remote. "In the car, we shifted out, and then right back in. Today, we shifted out, I waited for the laneway to clear—they had a whole bunch of cops searching for us—and then we shifted back in. It feels as if almost no time has passed for me, too."

"And if someone had seen us . . . shift?" Jillian asked, her brain grasping the concept but refusing to accept it.

"What would they tell the police? We were there, and then we weren't? The cops would have assumed that we'd used the rear door to enter the apartment, and the witness hadn't seen us do it. We try not to let people see us use certain gifts, but sometimes it can't be avoided, or we're inadvertently observed. Those who tell the tales are dismissed as crazy." She picked up her fork and jabbed at her salad. "That's what happened to me."

"What do you mean?"

"It's how I first became aware of the gifts, though I wouldn't have called them that back then. I started to time shift—involuntarily. I thought I was going crazy, and so did my parents, when I made the mistake of telling them about it." Sam looked at the lettuce she'd pierced, then put down her fork. "Well, first they took me to a doctor because they thought I was experiencing blackouts. When they couldn't find anything physically wrong with me and I kept insisting that I wasn't blacking out, that I could feel my body and see my surroundings, it was off to a psychiatrist."

"But you were untrained. How could you see your surroundings?"

"You can see yourself, right?"

Jillian nodded.

"And you can see me, but you can't see your environment. That's what other Fledglings experience, too. But not me. For some reason, I could still see my surroundings, but not the events taking place."

"So what happened?"

Sam shrugged. "The psychiatrist diagnosed me with schizophrenia, my parents filled the prescriptions, and I refused to take the pills. Fortunately a Deiform found me before things got ugly."

"Jim?"

"No, Brian. You haven't met him yet."

"How many Deiforms are there?"

"Worldwide?" Sam pondered the question. "Around fifty. Four of us work out of the island." She frowned. "Three, now. Me, Brian, and Warren. Counting you, it'll be four again."

Jillian wasn't going to repeat herself. "How did Brian contact you?"

"At the time, I'd just started university. He caught up with me on campus and said he could explain what I was experiencing. He talked, I listened, I believed him, I trained."

"Just like that? Some strange man approached you when you were, what, nineteen, and you just believed him? You never thought he might be some dirty old man trying to take advantage of you?"

Sam chuckled. "First of all, Brian was in his late twenties, hardly what I'd call a dirty old man. Secondly, he could describe exactly what I was experiencing. He shifted with me. I knew he was telling the truth."

"What were you studying?" Jillian asked, compelled to anchor the conversation with reality every few minutes.

"Religious studies."

Despite Sam's and the Fellowship's claims, the answer surprised Jillian. Most religious studies types didn't carry a concealed weapon, couldn't pick a lock to save their lives, and obeyed the law.

"You probably think I'm some thug, that Brian helped me to see the light and use my nefarious skills for Good, rather than Evil," Sam said, perhaps seeing Jillian's bafflement on her face. "That wasn't how it was. I was a model kid. A model Christian. I was devoted to God. Still am. That's why it was so confusing for me, and for everyone. They figured I must have some type of mental problem. Why else would I suddenly go off the rails? I wasn't on drugs or anything. And I'd never touched a gun—or a lock pick—in my life."

"Roberta said you're a Christian cell, and there's a chapel on the island. Are you all Christians?"

"On the island? Yes. But the Fellowship isn't exclusively Christian. Each cell draws members from a particular religion."

"I'm not a Christian," Jillian pointed out.

"You were raised in the Christian tradition." Sam ignored Jillian's answering scowl. "By Christian, we don't mean only evangelicals. That's your background, not everyone's. I'm Anglican. Brian's Catholic. Warren believes in God, but he was never a church-goer. Other Christian cells have evangelicals in them, but you were called to us."

Jillian sipped her tea. Ironically, it sounded as if she was brought up in a stricter Christian household than Sam and her fellow Deiforms. "What about the dogs at Marsh's house?"

"We do have some rudimentary communication with animals."

"You're kidding me."

"No. Our gifts are all anemic forms of God's attributes and abilities. He's constantly outside of time. We can shift for short periods. He can fully communicate with animals. We can convey basic commands. He can speak with anybody. We can telepathically speak to other Deiforms who are within a short range of us. And so on."

A reflexive laugh died in Jillian's throat. As usual, she was certain that Sam believed her own words, that she was sincere. If Jillian was honest with herself, she found it difficult to explain away the day's events. *Keep it real.* "It must have been rough, not understanding what was happening to you, and then leaving your family."

Sam's face tightened. "I knew I had to train. It's what I was meant to do."

"Still." Jillian hesitated. "Do you miss them?

Sam blinked at her. "Sometimes. I can't help but wonder how they are."

"You never check up on them?"

"Only once. My sister was sixteen when I," she formed air quotes with her fingers, "died. She always wanted to be a vet. I asked Jeremy to find out if she changed her mind. She didn't." Sam met Jillian's eyes. "She's doing what she's meant to do, and I'm doing what I'm meant to do."

"Why did you ask Jeremy? I'm sure you could have found out what she's doing."

"Sure. And then it would have been, is she married, what's her address, and so on. I know when I need to be delivered from temptation."

"What's her name?"

"Alex. Short for Alexandra." Sam raised her brows. "Maybe they wanted boys."

Jillian smiled. "So you have no regrets whatsoever about leaving your family?"

Sam took her time answering. "Only one. I wish I'd taken the time to say good-bye. Not explicitly, of course. But I wish I'd said some things to my parents and sister."

"Why didn't you? Didn't you know when you were going to . . . leave?"

"Yes, but I was nineteen. When Brian said, 'You'll never see them again,' I guess I didn't quite grasp that at the time. I was focused on the immediate future, desperate for life to make sense again." She shrugged, but the tension in her voice belied her attempt to appear casual. "Fortunately I was a good kid, so that's the only regret I have to live with."

Jillian swallowed. "How did you die?" she asked softly.

"I drowned. Several witnesses saw me fall through the ice, including a new friend from my therapy group. Anita—one of us. The rescue team searched for days. Found one of my boots and my hat, but not my body. According to the experts, the current had swept me out to sea. I was assumed dead." The tautness in her face eased. "We usually use explosions, drowning, anything where we can get away with no body, or one that's difficult to identify. Most of us are declared dead right away. On occasion, we've been missing until a court declared us dead."

"Your parents must have been devastated," Jillian said without thinking.

Sam went rigid and bowed her head. "They were," she said quietly. "But I was called to leave them behind, and I did."

Jillian winced at the pain her insensitive words had caused. Sam was either a brilliant actress, or she was telling the truth. Jillian shifted in her seat; the photo in her back pocket jabbed into her behind. She could handle the group turning out to be a sham, but if Sam turned out to be a fraud, Jillian would lose what little faith she had in humanity. She wanted to be straight with Sam; her instincts said to trust her. If she couldn't trust her own instincts . . .

As she reached into her pocket, the anger that had simmered since she'd discovered the photo rose to the surface. By the time she tossed the photo onto the table next to Sam's plate, it was in full boil. "What the hell is that?" she snapped.

Sam peered down at it. "A photo."

"Don't bullshit me!"

"I'm not. It's a photo!"

Jillian reached across the table and jabbed the photo with her finger. "Who's in it?"

"I don't know."

"You don't know."

"No." Sam looked from the photo to Jillian, then back to the photo again. "Is it you?"

"Yeah, it's me! Why, Sam?" Tears sprang to her eyes. "Why the deception? Why?"

"Where did you get it? You couldn't have had it on you when you were in prison."

"Jim's. I found it in his Bible."

Sam grimaced. "Oh, shit."

"What? I wasn't supposed to find out that your group has stalked me since I was a child? Jim screwed up again? What?"

"Jim, Jim, Jim," Sam murmured, shaking her head. She looked up; concern sharpened her eyes. "Hey, I know finding this must have been a shock. But it's not what you think."

Jillian blinked back her tears. "Then what is it? Tell me. I need to trust you." She inwardly winced at her pleading tone.

Sam leaned back in her chair. "Roberta said that knowing would taint your decision to join." She placed her hand on her chest. "I said that not knowing would taint it, that you should know before you make a decision."

"Know what?" She braced herself.

Sam chewed her lip. "Roberta won't be pleased with me, but too bad." She leaned forward, pushed away her half-eaten meal, and rested her elbows on the table. "Jim investigated your father."

Jillian balled handfuls of her jeans in her hands. "What do you mean, investigated?"

"He got involved, contacted your father, tried to help him out of his mess."

Jillian pushed away from the table and marched from the kitchen. "Jillian!"

No, no, no! She covered her ears. She couldn't take this anymore, having everything she believed and thought she knew assaulted. From the moment Jim had called her, she'd lost control of her life. It was time to take it back. Sam and her freaking Fellowship could go to hell.

Chapter Thirteen

W̲HEN THE KNOCK at the door came, Jillian didn't know how long she'd sat cross-legged on the bed, staring into the darkness. The door opened. Light spilled into the bedroom. Sam stood silhouetted in the doorway.

"What do you want?" Jillian said hoarsely.

"To apologize."

"For what?"

"For not standing up to Roberta and making her tell you." She leaned against the doorframe. "When you turned up at the community centre, she should have pulled Jim and sent another Deiform. He blamed himself when your father died."

"When he blew his brains out, you mean."

Sam didn't respond.

Jillian cursed her curiosity. "Why did Jim blame himself? What happened? Why was Jim involved?"

"Can I come in?"

"Yeah." When Sam stepped into the room and reached for the light, Jillian quickly added, "Leave the light off." Her cheeks were still wet.

Sam snatched her hand away. "Okay." She tentatively stepped toward the bed, then sat at its end with her back to Jillian. "What do you know about your father's . . . fall from grace?"

Jillian gazed at Sam's back. "He was skimming money from the church's coffers. Don't laugh. I know psychologists could have a field day."

"That's all you know?"

Was Sam asking because there was more, or because she didn't know the details? When Jillian had looked up old copies of the newspapers, the only sin they'd reported was embezzlement. "The adults wanted to protect me. Did you know he killed himself in my bedroom—while I was in bed?" And Mom was at bingo, her only indulgence and the one night a week she had to herself. What a scene to come home to. Mom had never played bingo again.

"No. His file doesn't mention that. Neither does yours."

Jillian supposed that where he'd blown his brains out didn't matter.

"Jim probably knew, though. I wouldn't have had a reason to know anything about your father. But Jim caused a stir when he identified you as the Fledgling. Roberta was skeptical, at first. She called a meeting. I guess she wanted our opinions as to whether it was wishful thinking on his part."

Was that why a guest speaker had led the lunchtime service not long after Jillian had begun to attend? "Why did she think it might be wishful thinking?"

"Jim always blamed himself that you and your mother were left alone. It wasn't his fault, though."

"No?"

"No." Sam's voice was firm.

"Why did he blame himself, then? Where there's smoke, there's usually fire."

Sam twisted to look at Jillian, then straightened. "I never got a chance to talk to him about that aspect of it, but I gathered that he wondered whether he'd pushed your father too hard. He was close to brokering a deal that would have allowed your father to maintain some shred of dignity and protected numerous congregations from details they didn't need to know. But your father was a tortured man. He knew what he'd done was wrong. He knew he'd let everyone down. When he killed himself, maybe he thought he was doing what was best for you and your mother."

Would it have been easier to live with a father in prison, than with no father at all? Had he honestly believed that his death would spare his family humiliation? Hadn't he considered the guilt he'd dump on them? The questions. The feelings of inadequacy.

"Jim wasn't stalking you," Sam said, interrupting Jillian's thoughts. "Roberta told me he had trouble letting go after your father's suicide. He kept an eye on you, but not for long. He couldn't. He was needed elsewhere. But obviously your father's case haunted him. He must have been shocked when he met you at the community centre."

"Don't expect me to feel sorry for him."

"Don't make him out to be the bad guy," Sam retorted. "I told you before, we're not infallible, and Jim's actions may not have had anything to do with your father's death. Jim was trying to help him."

Now Jillian was certain there must be more. "Why? What was so bad that my father drew the attention of your group? I can't believe you'd get involved because someone's dipping their hand into the offering plates." Frustration clenched her jaw when Sam didn't answer. *Tell me!*

"Your father wasn't an evil man. He was a weak man who got himself into a situation that affected thousands of people in church congregations, and the situation would have been worse if all the details had come out. There could have been a real backlash against innocent religious leaders." Sam paused. "This is going to sound harsh, but your father's death accomplished what Jim's deal would have ensured. There was no trial. The media got only part of the story. We buried the rest."

"And my mother and I buried my father."

Her words hung in the air. Jillian's frustration increased. Apart from the tidbit that her father may have stolen from more than his own church, she hadn't learned anything new. Sam wasn't giving her details. She drew breath. "Exactly what—"

"My laptop is on in my bedroom. Your father's file just happens to be open on it. I'm going to heat up the rest of my dinner. You're welcome to join me—after maybe taking a detour into my room. Either way, I'll be in the kitchen. Take your time. But remember—once you've read the file, you can't undo what you know. Think it over first. You can always read it another time."

No, it was tonight, or never.

"Since we're sitting in the dark having an honest conversation, is there anything you want to tell me? Anything you think we should know before you join us?"

What would it take to get it through Sam's thick skull that she wasn't joining them? *I'm sick of this!* "You know, there just might be something you should know. But if I tell you, you'll probably stop helping me. You want honesty? Here it is. I'm using you to clear my name. I'm not going to tell you anything that might stop you from doing that, because it's all I care about."

When Sam's shoulders stiffened, Jillian regretted her bluntness. She and Sam would have been around the same age when Dad died. Jillian shouldn't take it out on her, but nobody else was here.

Sam stood. "Thank you for your honesty," she said, her tone neutral. "I'll be in the kitchen."

For five seconds, Jillian pretended that she wouldn't spring from the bed and rush to the laptop. She listened to Sam descend the stairs, then had to restrain herself from running into Sam's bedroom. She forced herself to walk. Any other time, she might have glanced around Sam's room to see if she'd unpacked anything that offered hints about her interests, but Jillian only had eyes for the laptop. It called to her, and she eagerly succumbed to its siren.

It took her twenty minutes to read the file, and half an hour to digest its secrets and summon the courage to face Sam. She splashed water on her face in the bathroom, then plodded downstairs and into the kitchen.

Sam looked up from a book.

Jillian swallowed and opened a cupboard. "I don't suppose there's any alcohol in the house?" She hadn't noticed a liquor cabinet.

"No."

"And I suppose turning water into wine isn't one of the gifts?"

Sam's mouth twitched. "No."

"Oh, well. I've never been a big drinker anyway."

"I think there's a tub of chocolate ice cream in the freezer."

"That works." Jillian retrieved tub, bowl, and scoop. "You want some?"

"Sure."

She filled a second bowl, added a spoon to it, and set it down in front of Sam. Then she lifted her own bowl. As much as she'd like to, eating her ice cream while leaning against the counter out of Sam's viewing range would be cowardly. She pulled out the chair across from Sam, who snapped her book shut.

Jillian read the title. "You're interested in history?"

"Some history. My family is originally from England."

Tudor history made sense, then. Jillian spooned ice cream into her mouth and watched Sam do the same. She wanted to talk about it, but didn't know how to start.

Perhaps sensing her dilemma, Sam resolved the problem for her. "Did you know about the women?"

"No. I should have. The money certainly wasn't coming to us." They'd lived in the same modest bungalow her parents had bought soon after they'd married, driven around in the same ten-year-old sedan, gone camping rather than to Europe or warmer climes, and handed over coupons at the grocery cash—a task Mom had entrusted to her, making her feel like an adult. If anything, tension over money had risen during that final year, along with her parents' voices. Jillian had spent more and more time shut away in her room with her dolls, wondering why Mom and Dad were always mad at each other. She'd always assumed that her mother hadn't known what Dad was up to. Had Mom grown frustrated because she couldn't understand why she had to make do with less money? Or had suspicion sharpened her tongue? Had she known everything?

"Given my line of work, you'd figure I'd have doggedly pursued where the money went." Instead, she'd read the old newspaper articles and cringed. "I guess I knew, inside, that I wouldn't like what I found."

"Do you regret reading the file?"

Jillian shook her head. "It was painful to read, but I needed to know." She swallowed some ice cream. "The law would have punished him for the money, but not for devastating and humiliating my mother."

"Having an affair isn't against the law . . . or, at least, it's not against man's law." Sam's brows rose. "See, there is a difference between God's law and man's law."

Point conceded. "Why didn't he take Jim's deal?" Jillian wondered aloud.

"Maybe he felt backed into a corner. Maybe he couldn't bear to face the court. Maybe he thought killing himself would prevent any of it from becoming public. Or . . . maybe he felt it was the best way to protect you and your mother. We'll never know."

As much as she'd like to think that Dad had believed he was doing what was best for his wife and daughter, more likely he'd died a coward, unable to face the punishment and scorn he deserved. Some of those "women" he'd bedded could barely be considered that. Eighteen, nineteen? Immigrants the church was supposed to be helping. Oh, and another pastor's wife thrown in for good measure. Jesus.

Anger and grief tightened her throat. While Mom had pinched pennies, Dad's "girlfriends" had dined at fancy restaurants and strutted around in expensive jewelry and designer clothing. Hadn't anyone wondered how they could afford it, or had they all decided to look the other way? It wouldn't do to rock the boat, after all. Everyone showed up in their Sunday best, sang the hymns, and said the prayers. Appearances were everything. No cracks, no dissent, no accountability. All those times she and Mom had gone on outings by themselves, while Dad attended a church meeting, or counselled some poor family. "Your father helps people. He gives people hope," Mom would say, when Jillian asked why Dad wasn't with them. *Really, Mom? Really?* Was that what banging a teenager in some grubby motel room did? Give hope?

Shit, she could feel another round of tears coming on. Sam was watching. Her cheeks hot, Jillian focused on her ice cream.

"How did you get into your line of work?" Sam asked.

She gripped the spoon. "I guess I wanted to make amends for something that wasn't my fault."

Sam frowned. "I'm not trying to psychoanalyze you. I'm asking out of interest. Did you know that's what you wanted to do when you were in school, or . . ."

"I was always interested in math." She must have inherited that from Dad. Lucky her! "So I figured accounting might work. I got into university on a scholarship, and I won a couple of competitions. My grades were near perfect. That drew the attention of the agency. Then they investigated my background and decided I wasn't a good candidate, after all, especially when the psychologist doing my psych eval got wind of it. His bullshit report almost derailed my career before it got started."

"Children shouldn't pay for the sins of their fathers."

"It's a nice sentiment—in theory." Jillian scooped out the last of her ice cream and dropped her spoon into the bowl. "I didn't know about the agency's waffling when it was going on. I learned later that a couple of people, including my current boss, still wanted to recruit me."

"You mean Keller, right? You said you've always had a good working relationship with him."

Jillian nodded. "He and Jamieson, another department head, eventually got their way, but I always felt I had to work twice as hard as everyone else, and be perfect. One slip, and they'd accuse me of following in my father's footsteps."

"That's why you drove yourself so hard?" Sam studied her. "According to your file, you lived other lives more than your own."

Jillian narrowed her eyes. "You sure you're not trying to psychoanalyze me?" Then she shrugged. "I'd started to question whether I was losing myself. That's why I didn't fight the psychologist when she brought up a stint on desk duty." Had they really arrested her less than a week ago? It felt like a lifetime had passed. "I want this over with."

Sam understood what she meant. "I talked to Jeremy while you were upstairs. He and Emma are done. We should be able to complete our part tomorrow and pull the trigger the day after."

"So we'll plant the evidence at Donaldson's tomorrow?"

"Yeah, we caught a break. He left town today for a three-day conference. His mistress might be home, but it's a big house, and I doubt she'll be hanging out in his study. Everything we need, for Donaldson and setting it all in motion, will be delivered here tomorrow morning."

"You mean, it'll all be over in two days?" Two days, and she'd be free.

"Three. We'll set the plan in motion in two, but you won't be off the hook until the day after that—assuming everything goes well."

"What's the plan?"

Sam's forehead creased. "Let's talk about that tomorrow. I think we've had enough revelations for one day."

Anxiety snaked through her. Was Sam worried that she'd balk at the plan?

Sam lifted her book's cover, revealing the photo of Jillian. She handed it to her. "This is yours."

Jillian stared at it. "I'm sorry for being harsh with you upstairs. You had nothing to do with this."

"Apology accepted."

"Can I read *my* file?" she asked, looking up at Sam.

"Sure—when we're back on the island." Sam held up her hand. "I know, you're not going back. There's still time for you to change your mind, but not much time. Roberta wants a decision before we pull the trigger."

"Why? If I say no, will you suddenly decide not to go through with the plan after all?"

Sam pointed at her. "We've accommodated everything you've wanted. We haven't forced you to train. We're clearing your name. We're punishing Donaldson. It's time for you to give us a little something—to give us a show of faith, so to speak. We've put together a decent plan, but things can go wrong. We'd like a commitment from you before we put the plan into motion. We want to know that your willingness to join us doesn't depend on whether the plan works. If it does work, great, your name is cleared and we'll go back to the island. If it doesn't, it'll be unfortunate, but we'll have tried, and we'll go back to the island."

"You're both so damn sure I'll join you," Jillian said.

Sam rose and tucked the book under her arm. "You've already joined us, Jillian. You just haven't figured that out yet. But you will."

"Then why ask me for a decision? Why not drag me back to the island?"

"You must come willingly, and you will." Sam tapped her book. "I'm going to lounge on the sofa and read for a while."

Part of Jillian wanted to scream at her. The other part was growing dangerously attached to her. Was that the plan all along? To worm her way past Jillian's defences, earn her trust, form a bond, be a confidante and friend?

She peered at the photo she still gripped in her hand. The happy kid riding her brand new bike because she knew Mom wanted her to smile and laugh; the teenager toiling away in the library after school and shut in her room on Friday and Saturday nights, playing the role of straight-A student so she could avoid parties, dances, and dating;

the adult who felt more at ease in other people's skins than in her own—except for the past few days.

Ever since waking up on the island, she'd been herself. Sure, she'd gone along, curious to see how things played out. But she'd never pretended to share their beliefs. She hadn't told them what they wanted to hear, hadn't played the role of someone she wasn't. She'd been brutally honest with Sam. Her reputation, job, money, family . . . everything, stripped away. But rather than wallowing in the despair and emptiness left behind, she'd rediscovered the most valuable thing in the world: herself. *Underneath all the crap, I've always been here, and I'm not so bad after all.*

A lump rose in her throat. With Sam, she was herself. If she shared their beliefs, she'd be tempted to join them. Living in the same honesty she'd used with Sam, because they'd demand no less, would almost be worth leaving Mom and Danny behind. When she made the obligatory semi-annual pilgrimage to see them, Mom spent most of it watching TV. Hell, she and Mom hadn't had a meaningful conversation in years. They'd cope without her while she fought on behalf of Good. Hadn't she always imagined herself as the good guy keeping the bad guys in check?

But there was no point in considering it. She didn't share their beliefs. For the first time since meeting them, Jillian wished she did.

SLUMPED ON THE living room sofa, Jillian rubbed her eyes and yawned. She'd tossed and turned all night, her mind relentlessly torturing her with the details in Dad's file. Questions, disbelief, revulsion . . . She needed to forget about Dad and focus on the day ahead.

Sam walked in, carrying a box. Jillian straightened, grateful for the shot of adrenaline. "Are you going to tell me the plan now?"

Sam plopped the box on the coffee table. "Sure."

Jillian listened as Sam described their final tasks and how they'd bring the trail they'd laid to the attention of the authorities. "I'm not comfortable implicating Jim," she said when Sam finished.

"We have to give Donaldson a motive for killing him that makes sense. We know their real motive for killing him, but we can't explain that to the police, can we?"

No, insisting that Beguilers had killed Jim and Joanna, then framed her, would only lead to a different type of cell and a straitjacket.

Sam folded her arms. "Jim and Donaldson were partners in crime and had a falling out. Donaldson assumed that Jim's fundraising for his lunchtime church was a front for something else, so he sent you to investigate—not because he intended to prosecute, which would backfire on him, but to give him dirt he could use as leverage with Jim. But you couldn't find anything, and Jim figured out who you were working for. He called you, claiming he could prove that Donaldson was dirty. When you told Donaldson about the call, he decided to kill Jim and frame you. Your background made you vulnerable."

"Yeah, I can just hear him now: 'If I knew attending the services would make her flip, I wouldn't have chosen her for the operation.'" Jillian tried not to sound bitter, but didn't succeed.

"Exactly."

"I don't know, Sam. How can I sully Jim's name to clear mine?"

"Jim Preston never existed. He was a fabrication, his background made up. The real Jim would want us to do whatever we could to get you out of this mess. You know that."

Jillian slowly exhaled.

"He's not with us anymore. I admire your principles, but throwing your life away to protect a dead fictitious persona doesn't make a lot of sense."

"I suppose you're right. And I suppose Joanna was in the wrong place at the wrong time," she said, recalling that idiot lawyer Trotter's remark.

"Yeah." Sam opened the box and pulled out three envelopes, each with a removable label attached to it. "Perfect. One for the authorities, one for Donaldson's place, and one for Keller. Ready to go to the bus station?"

Jillian nodded. Sam dropped the Donaldson envelope back into the box and tucked the other two under her arm.

"What if Keller doesn't go along with it?" Jillian asked.

Sam looked at her. "Do you think there's a good chance of that happening?"

"I'm an accused double murderer on the run. But if anyone will hear me out, he will." She paused. "If I can get as far as telling him about the envelope, he'll check it."

"That's all we need. If what's in here," Sam glanced down at the envelopes under her arm, "doesn't pass muster, the plan fails."

"He might call the cops right after he hangs up."

"Let him. When they see what's in his envelope, they'll make him call you for the rest. At that point, you'd proceed as if he hadn't called them."

"And if he doesn't give me a chance to tell him about the envelope?" Jillian asked, wanting to cover all the bases.

"Then we'll find another way. We'll deal directly with the authorities if we have to, but it would be better to get Keller on your side and have him do it."

"Why not have someone drop off the envelope at a police station?"

"Because the police will ask too many questions. They won't just take the envelope and say thank you."

"We could mail it."

Sam shook her head. "They'll want to find the person who sent it."

Jillian lifted her hands. "Okay, okay."

"If we have to deal directly with the authorities, we will, but it's a last resort." Sam stuck her thumb over her shoulder. "Let's go."

They'd been in the car five minutes when Sam murmured, "We're being followed again. Interesting." At the next red light, she pulled out her phone and arranged to meet someone in a coffee shop's parking lot. By the time they got there, their contact was waiting for them. "It's Bill," Sam said as she lowered the car window.

Bill stooped and peered into the car. "What do you need me to do?" he asked.

"There are two envelopes in that bag." Sam pointed over her shoulder at the backseat. "I want you to go to the bus station and put each envelope into its own locker. Now, listen—this is very important."

Bill leaned closer.

"There's a label on each envelope. I need to know which key belongs to which envelope, okay? We can't screw that up. And take the labels off the envelopes."

"Got it."

"We have a tail. I don't know if they'll stay with us, or go with you. Don't let them see you at the bus station."

Bill opened the back door and grabbed the bag.

"Can you bring the keys to the safe house by eight?" Sam said. "I'll feel better if I have them before we move on to the next step."

"Will do."

"Thanks, Bill." Sam drove out of the parking lot and checked the rearview mirror. "The tail is sticking with us."

"Good," Jillian said.

"Not necessarily. It means they're focused on you." Sam chewed her lip. "The sooner you're back on the island, the better. I don't suppose you could give me your decision now?" Her eyes remained fixed on the road.

Jillian hesitated. When it came to the subject of her joining the Fellowship, she'd always been honest with Sam and wouldn't start lying to her now, even though her answer would make her vulnerable. "No. I haven't decided yet."

JILLIAN LOOKED ON from the sofa as Bill dangled two keys in front of him. "I wrapped the labels around them." He dropped the keys into Sam's palm.

"Good thinking," Sam said. "Did you have any trouble?"

Bill shook his head. "Did you? I noticed them going after you."

"No, nothing." They stared at each other. "Well, thanks for taking care of the envelopes," Sam said. "We're off to visit Donaldson's place."

After a moment, Bill asked, "Do you want me to tag along?"

"Yeah, why not?"

Rather than reassuring her, Sam's ready acceptance of Bill's offer unsettled Jillian. If Sam thought she might need help . . . Her anxiety increased when Sam said, "You armed?"

Bill lifted his jean jacket, revealing a pistol in a holster.

"I'll do the same, and so will you," she said to Jillian. "The armory's in the basement."

Jillian's feeble protests about strapping on a gun fell on deaf ears. When she climbed into the sedan's passenger seat, she was acutely aware of the holster pressing against her side. Sam handed her the envelope containing the pieces of evidence they'd plant at Donaldson's. Jillian hadn't asked what the envelopes contained, but based on her earlier conversation with Sam, she could guess that the one for Donaldson implicated him in setting her up and connected him to Jim, bolstering the contents of Keller's envelope. The envelope the authorities would find in the locker—assuming everything went according to plan—would clinch it.

Sam started the car, then turned to Jillian as the garage door opened. "Do not hesitate to protect yourself."

"I haven't used a gun since training."

"Point and shoot, Jillian. You don't have to kill them, just slow them down."

They drove out onto the driveway, waited until the garage door had closed, then turned onto the street. A pair of headlights appeared in the rearview mirror. "Bill," Sam murmured. A minute later, her phone rang. "Yeah." She listened. "There's no point in you trying to lead them away. They'll stick with us." Another pause. "Let's see how it plays out. I'd rather we get whatever they're planning out of the way, so if it's going to be tonight, it'll be tonight. If nothing's happened by the time we're approaching Donaldson's, I'll call you." She hung up. "They're behind Bill."

Jillian tensed. The gun strapped to her felt like a ton weight. She didn't accept that the Beguilers were Satan's agents, but that didn't mean she wasn't in danger. The Fellowship's enemy didn't have to be serving a supernatural master to kill her, but why would they want to? Was it a matter of picking off new recruits to prevent the Fellowship from growing?

When they were an exit away from Donaldson's, Sam's phone rang again. "Really?" she said. "Maybe they followed the wrong SUV off the highway. Or maybe they figured out where we're going and don't care. Thanks for letting me know."

"The tail is gone?" Jillian said.

Sam nodded.

"You'd think they'd care that we're going to Donaldson's."

"He's expendable. All they care about now is getting their hands on you. That's what it's always been about for them."

She had a target painted on her back. If she hadn't gone to Donaldson after Jim had called her, would any of this have happened? Would Jim have eventually left her alone and Donaldson been none the wiser? But she'd had no choice. With her cover blown, she couldn't have continued the operation. She'd had to tell Donaldson. Maybe she should have left the conversation with Jim out of it and claimed that she desperately needed to go on desk duty ASAP, that the psychologist was right, she was starting to crack.

But, come on! She hadn't taken Jim seriously—who would have? He should have told her that he worked for a criminal organization that wanted to recruit her, and not to run to Donaldson because he was dirty, too. That would have given her pause. She might have talked to Keller—who would have pooh-poohed her. She could hear his voice: *"Oldest ploy in the book, Jillian. Somehow Preston made you, and now he's trying to save the situation by bringing you over to his side. Don't let him turn you against your own people. Tell Donaldson."*

Yep, she would have ended up in Donaldson's office anyway. Sam was right. The moment Jillian had walked into the community centre, she'd inadvertently set into motion the events that had led to two people's deaths and spun her own life out of control. Considering Jillian expendable, Donaldson had intended to use her from the word go. Any lingering doubts she had about breaking into Donaldson's house and framing him died. The bastard deserved to rot in prison.

As for the Fellowship, the Beguilers, everything that had happened to her since waking up on the island . . . she didn't know what to believe anymore.

Chapter Fourteen

JILLIAN LET OUT her pent breath when Sam turned onto the ramp leading to the highway and accelerated. Good-bye, Donaldson. Planting the evidence had gone off without a hitch. No sign of any gifts, just the good old-fashioned method of disarming the alarm and creeping around in the dark, with the flashlight beam casting an eerie glow. Sam's sketches had turned out to be accurate, but she could have gotten photos from Jeremy, or maybe the house had come fully furnished and the rooms had appeared on a real estate website for all to see. Sam's drawings were easy to explain away. The time shifting—not so much. But scientists would probably explain it in the future. How many natural phenomena had once been attributed to gods, or even magic?

Fortunately, Mistress Donaldson hadn't been home. Maybe while the cat was away, the mouse was playing. Well, Mistress Donaldson would have to find herself a new sugar daddy, so if she was auditioning new candidates, good for her. Hopefully she'd settle on an unmarried one next time. "I feel sorry for his wife."

Sam glanced at her. "Donaldson's?"

"Yeah. Not only will she find out that her husband's a murderous bastard, but it'll probably come out that he had a play house and a bimbo."

"It'll be rough, but we're doing her a favour."

"I'm not sure my mother would agree with you."

"What about you?"

Jillian moistened her lips. "I prefer the truth, even when it hurts, but I don't know about my mother. I don't know if life would have been better for her—for us—if my father hadn't killed himself, but gone to prison. It's a waste of time to wonder about it."

"But you do."

"Not as often as I used to." Jillian gazed out the passenger window. "Is Bill still with us?" He'd remained outside while they'd tied Donaldson's noose.

"He pulled in behind us when we turned off Donaldson's street. He's a couple of cars back right now."

Jillian grunted, then turned to peer through the windshield when Sam slowed down. Brake lights were coming on. Up ahead, flashing lights. *Shit.* Jillian dug her fingers into Sam's arm, then relaxed them when she realized what she was doing. "Is it the police? If they're doing a spot check for drunk drivers . . ."

"They're not stopping people. It looks like they're redirecting everyone off the highway. There must be an accident."

Even so, Jillian wished she had the baseball cap. As Sam slowly followed the car in front of her onto the exit ramp, Jillian slumped down and bowed her head, as if she'd nodded off.

A minute later, Sam groaned. "Wonderful." The car stopped.

Jillian's heart pounded. She kept her head down. "What is it?"

"Now we've hit a construction zone. Two-lane road and only one lane is open. Some guy is letting a few cars through at a time." She sighed.

"I bet they're getting a lot of overtime for this."

Sam's phone rang. "Yeah." Silence. "I don't like it, but there's nowhere for me to go at the moment. Be ready." She hung up.

Jillian couldn't resist lifting her head. "What's going on?"

"Bill says the highway opened up again after the car behind him exited."

"Maybe it's coincidence. We don't know how long it was closed," Jillian said hopefully.

"It wasn't closed when we were on our way to Donaldson's." Sam's lips compressed into a thin line. "Be ready to use that gun. And be ready to hang onto something. I might have to floor it."

The sedan inched forward. The headlights of the car in front of them illuminated a man in a standard reflective construction vest and hard hat. He waved that car through and motioned for Sam to proceed. She looked at the rearview mirror as she drove around the truck blocking the lane. "He let the car behind me through, too."

"That's good, isn't it? Nobody's trying to isolate this car."

Sam didn't respond. The car accelerated. The trees lining the rural highway whipped by. Jillian breathed easier.

"Something's wrong!" Sam snapped.

"What—"

"There's no traffic on the other side! Hold—"

A loud bang drowned out Sam's words. Jillian lunged forward; her seatbelt dug into her.

"Shit!" Sam stepped on it. The car behind them kept pace and rammed them again.

Light suddenly assaulted Jillian's eyes. A car was in their lane, heading right for them! "Sam!"

Sam jerked the steering wheel to the right. Tires squealed. The sedan careened off the highway and into the brush. Trees hurtled toward the windshield. Jillian screamed. *Boom!* She flew forward, then back against the seat. Silence.

Disoriented, Jillian instinctively moved her arms and legs. Everything worked. The deployed airbag was deflating. Her brain kicked into gear. "Sam?" she croaked.

Sam coughed and waved away the dust swirling in the air. The sound of an engine broke the silence. Her arm stilled. "We need to get out of this car." She unlocked the doors.

Jillian unbuckled her seatbelt. Two cars pulled up, flanking them. Doors slammed. Sam reached for her gun. Someone jerked open the passenger door. "Hold on—" The driver's window shattered, spraying broken glass into the car.

Before Jillian could reach for Sam, strong hands grabbed her right arm and dragged her from the car. Pain shot through her shoulder; she landed on her back. Her heart raced; her mind screamed at her to get up and run as fast as she could. A hard-faced woman approached Jillian, the beams from her car's headlights casting an uncanny aura around her. She stood over Jillian and stared at her with dead eyes. "Get her on her feet."

Two men in dark coats gripped Jillian's arms and hauled her upright. Facing Sam's totalled car, Jillian could make out shadowy figures moving near the driver's side. "Let me see her," the woman said. The men holding her arms spun her around.

A gunshot from behind her, then another one. *Sam!* The woman giving orders nodded for the two men to step aside. She sneered and took Jillian's face in her hands. "Hello, Jillian. So nice to finally meet you."

JILLIAN COULDN'T HELP but grin when the pianist at the grand piano finished the piece from *The Sound of Music*. She'd lost count of how many times she'd sat enraptured in front of the TV, watching the Von Trapp family. The party guests rewarded the pianist with a smattering of applause, most too engaged in conversation to acknowledge his performance. Jillian wished she could do more than smile his way, but with a drink in her hand . . .

Someone tapped her on the shoulder. She turned away from the photographs on the wall. Cassandra's brother David beamed at her. "Cassandra hasn't stopped talking about your getaway together. I was quite astounded when I arrived tonight and saw this display." He swept his hand toward the photos. Jillian and Cassandra outside the Eiffel Tower; strolling along the Champs-Élysées; sampling the local cuisine . . . "I'm so pleased, for both of you, but especially for her. She's absolutely head over heels, Jillian. She's wearing her heart on her sleeve."

She blinked at him, then looked down at her wine. A single glass of red burgundy made from pinot noir grapes—her favourite—wouldn't cause the pleasant buzz she felt. Love was everything she'd expected, and more. "I'd always wanted to go to Paris. I'm so glad I waited until Cassandra came back into my life, so we could experience it together."

Gales of laughter rose from a group nearby. Jillian's nostrils flared. A good host didn't neglect her guests. This was Cassandra's house, but Jillian spent more time here than at her own penthouse condo, and Cassandra was throwing this soiree "to make sure that everyone important to me has met you, because you're going to be around for a long, long time." She hadn't come out and suggested that they move in together, but based on the hints Cassandra had dropped in Paris and since they'd returned, it was only a matter of time. Jillian couldn't wait. She touched David's arm and gave him her most dazzling smile. "I should circulate."

"Of course," he murmured. "So many are dying to meet you."

She sipped her wine and strolled over to the group that had caught her attention. Eyes lit up; several people quickly parted so she could join their circle. "What a wonderful party!" Annette, Cassandra's sister, said. "Everyone, this is Jillian Campbell." Over the rim of her glass, she coyly eyed Jillian. "We'll be seeing a lot more of her from now on."

The man standing next to Jillian stuck out his hand. "Michael Clark," he said as they shook. "Cassandra tells me you're an independent financial manager."

"That's right, I am."

A server walked by, balancing a silver tray laden with fruit on his shoulder. Jillian's mouth watered.

"I have some money I'm sure could be working better for me. I'd love to set up an appointment with you."

Jillian took in his neat haircut, tailored suit and tie, Rolex watch, gold pinkie ring, and leather shoes. He'd do. For the others . . . "I only work with elite clients, those with more than a million dollars to play with." She raised her brows. "At a bare minimum."

"Not a problem," Clark said over the whispers of the others.

A woman with a purse that cost more than most people made in a month lifted a finger. "I'd like to do business with you, as well."

"Of course." Jillian glanced around the room, caught Julia's eye, and beckoned her over. "This is Julia, my assistant. She'll be happy to set up an appointment with you and Mr. Clark—and anyone else who's interested."

"There you are!"

Warmth flooded through Jillian. Already grinning, she turned around. Her heart pounded, as it always did whenever Cassandra was near. Cassandra grabbed her arm. "Sorry, everyone, but I need to talk to my honey alone."

Jillian drained her glass and handed it to Julia.

"I'll bring her back soon, I promise." Cassandra squeezed Jillian's arm and steered her toward the hallway.

Jillian glimpsed herself in one of the full-length mirrors near the bottom of the staircase. Nothing boosted her confidence more than a designer business suit and kickass leather boots. Anthony had done wonders with her hair, too. She flicked it back, then giggled when Cassandra grasped her hand and pulled her up the stairs. "I can guess where we're going."

Sure enough, Cassandra led her into the bedroom and shut the door. She pushed Jillian against the wall and melted into her. Jillian hungrily sought Cassandra's mouth and parted her lips. Heat surged through her. She pulled Cassandra's shirt from the back of her pants, slipped her hand underneath it and ran her fingers up Cassandra's soft skin until they reached her bra.

Cassandra drew away. "Save it for later, darling. I want to talk."

"Talk?" Jillian cleared her throat and consciously slowed her breathing. "What about?"

"Us." Cassandra leaned in again and ran her finger down Jillian's cheek. "You know I want to wake up with you every morning." She traced Jillian's lips, then turned away and walked to the bed. "We belong together."

Jillian pushed away from the wall. "Just say the word. I'm half moved in already." She had her own space in the dresser and walk-in closet, all her favourite toiletries and beauty aids were in the ensuite, and family photos sat on the nightstand on her side of the bed. She went over to them and picked up the framed photo of Dad.

"Your father was a damn hero," Cassandra said, her voice infused with admiration. "They should have done more than name a park and church after him. Not everyone would have taken a bullet for those kids."

"That was Dad for you," Jillian whispered. She put the photo down, not wanting to relive that awful night when the police had shown up at the door and solemnly informed Mom that Reverend Campbell had sacrificed his life to save two children during a convenience store holdup. The community and congregation had rallied, supporting Mom through that terrible first year, and generously donating to the trust fund that had put Jillian through university. Mom had grieved for Dad, then picked up the pieces, found a job, and married a co-worker who had custody of two children. Jillian had gained two stepsiblings, and her merged family had spent many happy Christmases and vacations together. They adored Cassandra almost as much as she did. "Mom would love to see us living together."

"So would I." Cassandra gazed at Jillian with her intense emerald eyes. "But there *is* one small matter to deal with before we take that step."

Jillian's heart felt as if it was leaping from her chest. "What?"

Cassandra smiled. She sashayed toward Jillian and rested her forearms on Jillian's shoulders. "I'm a jealous girl," she purred. "I wish I'd taken more notice when we were younger, so we hadn't wasted so much time."

Oh, so did Jillian. If she could turn the clock back . . .

"I understand that you dallied with other women, just as I did. We didn't know."

"No, we didn't," Jillian said.

"But now I want you all to myself. I don't want any reminders of your past life hanging around."

"What are you talking about?"

Cassandra's face tightened. "You know what—or rather, who—I'm talking about. That bitch who keeps coming between us. I want her out of our lives. Permanently."

Jillian's mind raced. "There is nobody. I wasn't in a relationship when we ran into each other." Blood rushed to all the right places when she remembered meeting Cassandra's eyes at the museum.

Cassandra tutted. "She's a crafty one, isn't she? You think she's a friend, because she acts that way. But she wants you. She can't stand the thought of us together. She will do everything in her power to keep us apart. She even came here tonight! Slipped through security and almost made it into the house. Can you imagine how humiliating it would have been for me to stand and watch another woman declare her undying love for you in front of my family and our friends?"

"Who is it?" Jillian asked indignantly. "I swear to you, I had no idea. Anyone who's trying to break us up is no friend of mine. I'll make sure she knows that she's not welcome in my life. I want to get rid of her as much as you do." Nobody would come between her and Cassandra.

Her breath caught in her throat when Cassandra softly kissed her on the cheek. "I was hoping you'd say that, darling. Carl has her in one of the guest bedrooms. Shall we go have a chat with her?"

"Yes." She took Cassandra's hand and interlaced their fingers. "How long have you known? If you'd told me earlier, I would have dealt with it."

Cassandra opened the door. "I thought I'd give you a chance to figure it out yourself, first. I don't like to interfere in your life, Jillian. But you weren't seeing it, and I'm tired of her lies about me."

They went into the second guest bedroom down the hall. Carl stood next to the bed.

"Bring her out where we can see her," Cassandra said as she closed the door.

Carl stepped aside and grabbed the shirt collar of the woman who knelt with her hands cuffed behind her back. He dragged her in front of Jillian and Cassandra, then grabbed her hair and pulled her head back.

A palpable sense of dread overwhelmed Jillian. She could hardly breathe. "Sam." One of Sam's eyes was swollen shut, angry red bruises covered both cheeks, and dried blood was caked underneath her nose and on her lips and chin. "Did you have to beat her?" Jillian asked, her eyes moving to the red stains on Sam's white shirt.

"If you'd heard the filth coming out of her mouth, you'd have wanted to beat the crap out of her, too," Carl said.

"But you did hear it, didn't you, darling?" Cassandra cupped Sam's chin. "What have you been telling her, Samantha? That I'll hurt her? That I'm not good for her? That you're trying to help her?" She drew back her hand and slapped Sam across the face. "You want her for yourself, don't you? You're the liar, you're the one who wants to hurt her. You'll do anything to have her to yourself, you self-righteous bitch. You're no better than anyone."

Sam whimpered.

"What's the matter? Cat got your tongue?"

Carl guffawed. Jillian swallowed, looking from Sam to Cassandra, then back to Sam. She tried to think. Her head hurt.

Cassandra held out her hand to Carl. "Give me your gun."

Carl reached under his jacket, pulled out a pistol, and passed it to Cassandra.

Jillian's legs turned to jelly when Cassandra flashed a smile. "You know what needs to be done, darling. There's only one way to permanently remove Samantha from our lives, and it needs to be you. I have to be able to trust you. Do this one thing for me, and we'll be together forever." She handed Jillian the gun. "It's me or her, Jillian. You can't have both."

Jillian gripped the gun with both hands and looked down at Sam. Cassandra wanted her to kill? If it was the only way . . . they did belong together, but . . . but . . . Something nagged at her, but her mind couldn't grab it. It was as if she had a word on the tip of her tongue, right in front of her, but just out of reach.

"I know I'm asking you to kill for me, but it will be merciful, Jillian. I'm afraid Carl went a bit too far when Samantha got on his nerves."

"What do you mean?" Jillian asked, her eyes still on Sam.

Carl tossed a bloody towel onto the bed and unfolded it, revealing a shrivelled tongue. Jillian's stomach lurched; bile burned her throat. The room spun. Dread clung to her like a wet blanket. The gun burned her hands.

"Put her out of her misery, darling." Cassandra's arms coiled around Jillian; her tongue slithered into Jillian's ear. "Show her mercy. Send her to her maker. You know she wants to go to her maker."

Jillian pointed the gun at Sam's head.

"Send her home, darling."

Her finger moved to the trigger.

"Say hello to your god for me, Samantha."

Sam cringed and turned her head away.

The scales fell from Jillian's eyes. She spun toward Cassandra and pulled the trigger, then dropped the gun when a horrific shrieking ripped through her mind . . .

JILLIAN STARED INTO cold, angry eyes. The woman dropped her hands from Jillian's face. "You stupid bitch." Hard metal jabbed into her stomach. "Good-bye, Jillian."

Pain tore through Jillian's abdomen. She stumbled backward. Her back hit the car; her legs went from under her. She slid to a sitting position.

The woman stepped toward her and raised her gun for another shot. Jillian defiantly met her eyes.

Blam, blam, blam!

Blood sprayed from the woman's arm and chest. She fell out of Jillian's field of vision. Someone in a dark coat leaped over Jillian's legs.

"Sam, two o'clock!" a man shouted.

More gunshots.

Why is it so difficult to breathe? What's wrong with me? Jillian clutched her stomach, then raised her trembling hand and stared in confusion at the blood.

Someone groaned. "I hope you're in as much pain as I am, darling. At least we won't die alone. We have each other."

Was she dreaming? *No, I'm dying.* Jillian rested her hand on her bleeding stomach, tilted back her head, and stared up at the stars, the beautiful, magnificent stars. She should have taken the time to look up more often. Why hadn't she taken the time? Why hadn't she lived? What had she been waiting for? Her heart, her precious heart, continued to pump blood from her body; she could feel her life draining away . . .

Something heavy thudded to the ground nearby. Running footsteps, then Sam's face swam in front of Jillian, blocking her view of the sky. When Sam crouched next to her, Jillian lifted her hand and tried to touch Sam's cheek, but her movements were jerky. Sam gripped Jillian's slippery hand.

"She's . . . still alive," Jillian whispered.

"It's okay. Bill's got her covered."

"I'm going to die."

"Not if I can help it. This is going to hurt." Sam tightened her grip; her eyes grew distant.

Jillian gasped; her body arched. She screamed . . . screamed . . . screamed. Every cell burned; white seething light; pain! Rattling her teeth . . . *Mercy! Please, have mercy! I can't take it. I can't . . .*

Cool, soothing, relaxing peace. She could breathe again, and let out a long, relieved sigh. Sam was still there, holding her hand. Her face ashen, she smiled weakly at Jillian.

"Will she be okay?" Bill's voice.

"Yeah," Sam said, her voice a thread. She squeezed Jillian's hand. "You'll feel weak, but you'll live."

Jillian braced herself and looked down. Her shirt and jeans were covered in blood, but the pain had dissipated and she could feel her strength returning. Bewildered, she lifted her eyes to Sam's. "She shot me in the stomach."

Sam nodded. "Yeah, a couple more minutes, and it might have been too late. I can heal, but I can't resurrect. I hate healing, though. It knocks the stuffing out of me."

Jillian blinked at her.

"Are you going to heal me, Samantha?" a raspy voice asked. A chill ran up Jillian's spine. Now that her head was clear, she recognized the voice. Cassandra.

Sam yanked her hand from Jillian's. "Bill!"

"Still got her covered."

Coughing, then, "Relax. I'm on my way out. Will you hear my confession, Samantha?"

Sam's face tightened.

"Don't deny me my confession, Samantha." Another cough. "I killed one of your precious Deiforms and his friend. You should have seen the terror in their eyes when I poured the gasoline and lit the match. Yes, they were still alive. It was so much more satisfying that way, and the marshmallows were delicious."

Sam stiffened and pulled out her phone.

"Oh, but Jimmy and I had a good time together before he died. I didn't have much trouble persuading him to donate his semen. Samantha, did you know that he called out your name while he was riding me? What *do* you get up to on that island of yours?"

"Hi, we ran into trouble," Sam said, her knuckles white. "I need to talk to Roberta. Now."

"You should really . . ." Wheezing. "You should really let your hair down, Samantha. Enjoy the fruits life has to offer. You're too uptight."

"Jillian's fine, but we have a dying Beguiler here. Lilibeth, I believe. She claims that she killed Jim and Joanna. What do you want me to do?"

"Are you calling mommy for permission? How sweet. You should drag me into the trees and leave me to slowly bleed to death. That's what I'd do if it were you, Samantha, though I'd strip you and have my way with you, too."

"You sure? Okay." Sam snapped her phone shut and pushed to her feet.

"What's the verdict?" Cassandra—Lilibeth—rasped.

Jillian turned her head to look.

"We're referring your case to a higher court." Sam stood over the woman, pulled out her gun, and shot her in the head. She stepped away. "We're done here. Bill, she might need help to the car." Sam holstered her gun as she strode past, her face like thunder.

Jillian tried to stand, but her legs weren't cooperating.

"Whoa!" Bill said, catching her. He supported her until she stood on shaky legs, then scooped her into his arms.

She clung to his neck as he carried her to the SUV, and stopped counting the bodies he skirted when she reached five.

Chapter Fifteen

WRAPPED IN A blanket on the sofa, Jillian sipped her tea and watched Sam pace with her phone to her ear. "They must have had more already on the way if they managed to clear most of the scene before anyone else arrived. It's a good thing we got out of there when we did." Sam listened. "No, from the time we crashed, we were there ten minutes, tops."

Ten minutes?

"I don't know why they left our car with Lilibeth's body in it. I'd say it's some type of message, but I don't see an obvious one. Maybe they figured it would cause confusion for the authorities. They might think it's a gang hit." She stopped pacing. "Yeah, I'll tell her. Talk to you tomorrow." She hung up and faced Jillian. "You feeling okay?"

Way better than she should. After convincing Sam that she was strong enough to take a shower without collapsing in the tub, she'd stood under the water and stared at her abdomen; pressed it; ran her fingers along its skin, looking for any sign that a bullet had ripped through it, tearing apart her insides. Bloody water had run down her legs and rushed toward the drain, mixed with her tears. Her blood-soaked pants and shirt—the latter with a bullet hole—were in the garbage. Yet here she was, lounging on the sofa, sipping tea. "Physically, I'm fine."

"But you're wondering what happened." Sam sat at the other end of the sofa and twisted toward Jillian.

"Were we really only there for ten minutes?"

Sam nodded.

"It felt like more than ten minutes."

"You were enchanted. It's like dreaming, except they control what you're seeing. Have you ever fallen asleep and dreamed for hours, then you wake up, check the clock, and only five minutes has passed?"

Jillian nodded, then sipped her tea when her eyes filled with tears. Somehow Lilibeth had dredged up fantasies Jillian hadn't had for years, desires she'd never, ever shared with anyone. She felt violated.

"I hear it's not pleasant," Sam said softly.

Jillian swallowed. "It's never happened to you?"

"No. And it never will. They can't do it to a trained Deiform. We've already made our choice."

"What do you mean?"

"From what I know, the enchanted is always asked to make a choice. It's how they turn Fledglings that haven't come in. It's why we contact Fledglings as soon as we can—except in your case." Sam's tone hardened. "I guess Lilibeth figured you weren't on the island long enough to train, so why not give it a try?"

"She almost succeeded." Jillian wanted to slap herself. How could she have been so stupid?

"Do you want to talk about it?" Sam held up her hand. "Given how personal enchantments can be, I'll understand if you don't want to."

Jillian took a deep breath. She needed to get it off her chest, no matter how bad it would make her sound. Sam had saved her life. How she'd done it was a mystery, but that she had was indisputable. Telling Sam about the sick little play she'd starred in could mean the end of Sam's help, but she no longer wanted to use Sam and the Fellowship. Her heart just wasn't in it—not after tonight. As far as Sam went, maybe it never had been.

She leaned forward to set her teacup on the coffee table, then shifted position and drew the blanket tighter around her shoulders. "I was at a party." She lifted her finger. "Which should have tipped me off right away, because I hate parties. When I was working a case, I'd nurse a single drink all night, while hoping alcohol, and sometimes drugs, would loosen everyone's lips. I always counted the minutes until I could get away." The odd time she was invited to one as herself, she'd stood awkwardly off to the side, or latched onto the first poor person who showed any interest. "But not at this party. Oh, no. I was Ms. Confidence. Had a glass of my favourite wine, the pianist was playing my favourite music, I felt like a million bucks in the clothes I was wearing. And frankly, I was an asshole."

Measuring people's worth by their clothes and accessories—how shallow and greedy could one be? She'd strutted around, putting on superior airs and enjoying every minute of it. Hell, if she'd gone to the bathroom, she probably would have crapped gold nuggets. "If these enchantments bring out your true nature, I'm not a very nice person."

"They don't. They twist. They magnify. They exploit."

"And I fell for it, hook, line, and sinker."

"Give yourself a break," Sam said. "Until you wake up, you believe what you're dreaming, even when you're doing and saying things you'd never do and say when you're awake."

Yes, but her dreams normally didn't indulge ridiculous childish fantasies. Dad, dying a hero, and Mom, marrying the perfect man and forming the perfect blended family. Honestly! She was surprised violin music hadn't soared out of nowhere when she'd gazed down at Dad's photo with trembling lips. And she'd fallen for it. Jesus.

Sam was watching her. "You figured it out when it counted."

Yes, and she was stalling, because now came the part that might sour her association with Sam and the Fellowship. A few days ago, she'd considered it the ace up her sleeve to throw onto the table if they refused to let her return to her life. Amazing, how much difference ten minutes could make. No, that wasn't entirely true. It wasn't only what had happened tonight. Sam's dedication, her . . . abilities . . . Jillian could no longer dismiss everything out of hand. She didn't share Sam's devotion to God; she didn't believe Sam's "gifts" came from some benevolent deity who cared about what happened to everyone on this crazy planet. But she could respect Sam's beliefs, and she accepted that Sam could do things that science couldn't explain—yet.

Jillian wished she hadn't put her tea down, because she'd sure appreciate something to focus on right now. She forced her eyes to Sam's. "When I was in high school, I had a crush on a girl named Cassandra. She was one of the in-crowd, and always surrounded by boys. I admired her from afar. I doubt she said more than a few words to me over the five years we were at school together, and those words were along the lines of, 'Get out of my way.'" She paused, in case Sam wanted to say anything, but Sam remained silent, her expression unchanged. "The party was at Cassandra's house, and we were a couple. She didn't even look like an older version of Cassandra, but somehow I thought it was her." *I'm so glad I waited until Cassandra came back into my life.* Came back into her life? Please.

"Was Cassandra the part Lilibeth played?" Sam asked.

Jillian nodded. "She asked to see me alone. We went upstairs. She told me she wanted me to move in with her, but I had to take care of a problem first, that someone was coming between us. It turned out to be you."

Sam snorted.

"From the moment I saw you, I just—I felt—something didn't feel right, but I still didn't understand that none of it was really happening." She hesitated. "You were badly beaten up. They'd cut out your tongue."

Sam's brows shot up. "They cut out my tongue?"

"Yeah. And your attitude . . . something was off. I think that's why I finally came to my senses. You would have been defiant. You would have struggled, or tried to communicate with me somehow. But you just knelt there."

"Oh, so I was on my knees, too." Sam shook her head. "Lilibeth just couldn't help herself. She had to inject her own fantasies, and that turned out to be her downfall."

"You're right." Jillian's hands clenched when she thought about what happened next. "She handed me a gun and told me it was you or her."

"The choice."

"Right. I didn't want to shoot you. I could sense that my mind was trying to tell me something. I couldn't believe she wanted me to kill for her, but I pointed the gun at your head. And she said, 'Say hello to your god,' or something like that, and you cringed and shied away." A lump formed in Jillian's throat. "You would never have done that. You would have stared down that barrel and dared me to send you to your Lord. So I knew, without a doubt, that it wasn't you, and that broke the illusion. Suddenly I was back outside the car, and she shot me." Jillian wiped her forehead with a shaky hand, then hung her head, humbled and ashamed.

"You've made your choice. They can never do that to you again."

"I wish I could forget it."

"No, it'll come in handy when you need to remind yourself of why you left your life behind."

"Sam . . ." Jillian raised her head. "The crush I had on Cassandra in high school . . . it wasn't a phase."

Sam's mouth turned up at the corners. "You won't be the first gay Deiform, and I'm sure you won't be the last. I'm glad you finally told me."

"You knew?"

"It's in your file."

Shock stabbed through Jillian. "How can it be in my file? Nobody knows except me." Okay, she'd had a relationship while she was in university, but it hadn't lasted long. She hadn't been ready to come out, and since then, it had been work, work, work. "There's no way you could know."

"Roberta knew."

God told her? Or had the Fellowship somehow found out from Amy? No, that didn't make sense. How would they know to ask her? "Why didn't you say anything?"

Sam shrugged. "I wanted to see if you'd tell me."

"You knew when you asked me about the semen report."

"Yes, I did. That was the first opening I gave you to tell me, but you didn't bite. I figured we needed to build a greater level of trust between us first." She chewed her lip. "I was in the middle of working on something when Roberta called me in to train you. She knew I wouldn't be happy about turning it over to Brian, and I wasn't. I didn't understand why she insisted it be me until I read your file. Roberta's an astute woman. She anticipated that you might use your sexuality as an excuse to not join us. What better way to counter that than to call in a gay Deiform to train you?"

Jillian had to consciously prevent her mouth from falling open. God himself appearing right here in the living room was the only revelation that would shock her more. Sam was gay? Jillian had noticed that she wasn't a girly girl, but she'd thought—she'd assumed—okay, another preconceived notion about the Fellowship had flown out the window.

"Never underestimate Roberta. I know you think she's deluded, but you'll learn when to argue and when to do exactly what she tells you to do. Like give her a decision by tomorrow afternoon."

"Do I have a choice? You always talk as if I've already agreed to return to the island with you."

Sam grimaced. "They won't stop coming after you. We've slowed them down. It'll take them time to regroup. But if you don't join us, they'll try again, and since you'll be out here on your own, they'll succeed. They'll kill you."

A few days ago, Jillian would have scoffed, but not anymore. "What were you working on when Roberta called you in?"

Sam's eyes narrowed. "Why do you want to know?"

"Because I need more information. You told me about Jim and my father. I accept that a group with members who can . . . I don't know, control minds . . . opposes you. But what do you normally do? I assume you don't spend all your time butting heads with Beguilers." That would be pointless.

"Very little time, actually. It mainly happens when a Fledgling appears."

"Did they come after you?"

"They didn't have time. Roberta was quick, maybe because I was younger than usual."

"So what were you working on?" Jillian asked again.

Sam rubbed her finger along her lower lip. "I can't give you details. It was—still is—a large-scale sexual abuse case. I was gathering . . . data when Roberta called me in."

"Were you going to stop it?"

"And expose it."

"Why that particular case? It's happening everywhere. Why aren't you stopping every case?"

"Why aren't you?"

Fair point.

"We can't do it all. We have to focus on the bigger picture. That's not always easy, but it's what we do," Sam said.

Jillian blew out an exasperated sigh. How could they expect her to join them blind? Or was that the intent? She had to join "on faith." Okay, she wasn't completely in the dark, but she wished she knew more.

"Sometimes we help. Sometimes we hinder. It depends on the situation," Sam said.

"Give me an example."

Sam took her time answering. "Sometimes we prevent an assassination. Sometimes we stand by and let it happen. Sometimes we might help one along."

"Based on what? What Roberta says?"

"Not entirely, but she usually sets the general direction."

Jillian was about to snap, "You're playing God," then realized how ridiculous that would sound. Of course they were playing God. Jesus. "I believe that *you* believe you serve God. Even if I believe in the same . . ." she searched for an appropriate word, "values, or goals, or bigger picture, that you do—right triumphing over wrong and ensuring that Evil doesn't run circles around Good—I don't believe in God. I can't join you."

Sam studied her. The silence—a comfortable one—stretched out. "Let me ask you a question," she finally said.

Instantly on her guard, Jillian waited.

"If someone gives a meal to a hungry person, do you think it matters to that person whether that someone provided the meal because she's compassionate and believes in God, or because she's compassionate, full stop? Does it matter?"

"You think it matters."

"Do I? And that's not what I asked."

"Aren't you supposed to be trying to convert me?"

"Am I? You still haven't answered the question," Sam countered.

Jillian folded her arms. "No, it doesn't matter, but what's your point? It doesn't change the fact that you're asking me to join a group in which everyone has given up everything to serve something I don't believe in."

"You don't believe in the greater good? In right triumphing over wrong? In, uh, Evil not running circles around Good?" Sam leaned forward. "You don't have to believe in the same way we do. You only have to believe in what we do. Those kids in that sexual abuse case? When we stop it, because we will, do you think they'll give a shit about what we believe? The only thing that will matter is that we stopped it. Well, they won't know it was us, but you know what I mean."

It would be easier if she didn't.

"Words, creeds, are easy. Actions count."

Sam was preaching to the choir, which irritated the hell out of Jillian. Churches were filled with hypocrites. "This all sounds great in theory, until Roberta orders me to kill someone because God told her to." Wincing, Jillian cursed her insensitivity. "I'm not—I wasn't thinking about you killing Lilibeth. If I'd had the strength, I would have dragged myself over there and shut the bitch up myself, ordered to by God or not."

Weariness etched on her face, Sam ran a hand through her hair. Jillian's desire to verbally spar with her, to make her explain and defend her beliefs and her choices, drained away. They'd both had a hell of a night. "Look, we're only going to go around in circles. You said you want a decision by tomorrow afternoon. You'll have one."

Sam nodded. The fight seemed to have gone from her, too.

"How are you feeling?" Jillian asked.

"I've had better nights. I'll be happy to get back to the island. It's the only place I can let my guard down." Sam pushed herself up from the sofa. "I'm going to bed."

"Sam," Jillian called when Sam reached the bottom of the stairs.

She turned.

"I don't know how you did it, but thanks for saving my life."

"I didn't save your life, Jillian. I was the conduit, nothing more." Sam put her hand on her hip. "Doesn't the fact that I healed you," *"and can speak to you like this,"* "make you think that maybe there is something—or someone—out there?"

"The fact that I can't explain it doesn't prove the existence of God. Maybe your gifts come from aliens. Maybe you have a rare mutation that only occurs in fifty people in the world. There could be hundreds of explanations. God doesn't have to be the default one." When Sam didn't react, Jillian said, "Can I ask you a question?"

"Sure."

"Did you mean it when you said that your only regret is not taking the time to say a proper good-bye to your family? You were totally okay with leaving everything behind at nineteen?"

Sam's brow furrowed. "Yeah. What we do is important. It matters. I'm called to do it." She paused. "And so are you. Good night."

Jillian listened to her climb the stairs, then reached for her tea and gulped down the rest of the lukewarm liquid. Maybe the Beguilers wouldn't come after her. They knew she wasn't trained. If she didn't return to the island, maybe—no. They'd kill her out of spite, or because of her role in Lilibeth's death, or because it might offend the Fellowship—maybe all of the above. So, what were her choices? Join a group whose ideals she could morally and intellectually agree with, but in which she'd always be the odd one out, no matter what Sam said. And then there was Mom and Danny . . . Or, live on borrowed time, constantly looking over her shoulder, but there would be a body for Mom and Danny to bury—hopefully—and she'd die living the life she'd chosen to live, should that be her choice. If she joined the Fellowship, it couldn't be to save her ass. It would have to be what she truly wanted to do with her life.

If the past week had taught her anything, it was that she'd led a pathetic existence. Sure, she'd helped to bring white-collar criminals to justice. But she'd been sleepwalking, using Dad's suicide as an excuse to avoid living. He'd killed himself, and so had she. Unlike him, she had a second chance at life, and she wouldn't squander it. If she remained in the "real world," screw her job. When the Beguilers came for her, they'd find her working to make the world a better place, not chasing down missing dollars for some fat-cat corporation. She wouldn't waste any more time being someone she couldn't stand. From now on, she'd strive to make every minute of her life reflect her principles, and she'd spend her time with people who shared those principles. So let the Beguilers come for her. She'd die knowing that she'd started to turn her life around. Her only regret would be that she hadn't had more time to—

She almost dropped the cup she still clutched. Rarely had an epiphany slapped her across the face so hard, but she'd spent the last god knows how many years avoiding any real thought about her life.

Chapter Sixteen

J ILLIAN CHUCKLED TO herself as she flipped through the TV
channels, sure that Mom was probably sitting in front of the TV at
that very moment, doing the same thing. She stopped on a 24-hour
news channel and glanced at the digital clock in the corner—*16:31*—
then quickly flicked away, not wanting to see any reports about the
dead woman found in a car the previous evening. Sam had assured
her that the authorities wouldn't trace the car to them or the safe
house, and Jillian didn't want to dwell on it. Nope, she was content
to sit in a trance and watch mindless shows.

After lunch, Sam had gone down to the basement, apparently
to review every shred of evidence Jeremy and Emma had planted.
But that wouldn't take all afternoon. Jillian suspected that Sam had
taken the opportunity to put her feet up and read. She seemed to
need time alone today, to decompress after last night. If they were
friends, maybe they'd talk about the aftershock, flash back together,
and remind the other that they'd survived and made the right choices.
Instead, they'd isolated themselves, Sam retreating downstairs, and
Jillian lolling around on the sofa as if she hadn't a care in the world.
But the afternoon was almost over, and Roberta wanted a decision.
Had Sam not asked yet because she was busy, absorbed in a book, or
didn't want to know?

When Jillian heard footsteps thumping up the stairs at 4:50, she
pointed the remote at the TV and turned it off.

Sam strode into the living room and shoved her hands into her
pockets. "I have to call Roberta," she said, sounding almost apolo-
getic. "She wants you back on the island as soon as you're cleared,

which should be tomorrow, unless something goes wrong. Have you reached a decision?"

"Yes, I have. But let me ask you something first. If I decide not to join you, what will happen after they've dropped the charges and I've signed the immunity papers?"

Sam rocked on her heels. "You go back to your life."

She mentally thanked Sam for not pointing out that she wouldn't survive very long. "And if I join you?"

"You say good-bye to the lawyer and get into the car, we drive to the airstrip, and fly to the island. As soon as we're ready, we bring you back here to kill you."

"I couldn't see my mother and stepfather?"

"It's too late for that."

Jillian steeled herself and motioned toward the armchair. "Sit down."

Over an hour later, she watched Sam snap her phone shut and shake her head. "She's not happy," Jillian said. Probably the understatement of the year.

"No, she's not." Sam's eyes were bleak.

"Neither are you."

"No, I'm not. But I understand it." With a sigh, she stood. "Anyway, Bill will be here in an hour. Let's eat."

"Sam."

"What?"

"Thank you for talking to Roberta. I might have caved and done what she wanted."

Sam smiled weakly. "No problem."

Jillian couldn't bear the anxiety in Sam's voice and eyes. The poor woman looked as if she carried the fate of the world on her shoulders. "Why don't you go and read? I'll make dinner." To atone for being selfish, and for giving Sam the one reason she knew Sam couldn't counter. Jillian felt worse when Sam left the room without protesting. *I'm sorry.* She wished she could go along with what Roberta and Sam wanted, but she had to do what she honestly believed would be the best for everyone, including the Fellowship, long term.

Time to make dinner, and then to venture out to place the last puzzle piece and "pull the trigger," as Sam would say. If everything went well, Jillian would be back out in the real world this time tomorrow—and vulnerable.

SAM CLIMBED INTO the SUV's passenger seat and slammed the door shut. "Piece of cake." She pulled out her phone and held it out to Jillian, who was in the backseat. "You're on. His number's in there."

Jillian took the phone from her and found the number in the contact list. Bill lifted binoculars to his eyes. Every ring fuelled Jillian's heart rate. *Come on, Keller, pick up the damn phone.*

Finally, a click. "Hello?"

"Keller, it's Jillian. Don't hang up."

Keller's voice jumped an octave. "Jillian? Just a second." She heard the sound of a door closing, then, "Jesus, Jillian, where are you? What's going on?"

"I need your help. Donaldson's dirty."

"What?"

"Donaldson is dirty. He set me up. You don't seriously think I killed Preston and his associate, do you? Donaldson set me up. I can prove it."

Keller's breath whistled between his teeth. "Wait a minute, wait a minute. If you can prove it, call the police."

"The police will throw me into a cell first and ask questions later. Before I hand over what I've got, I want the charges against me dropped and immunity from further charges." Silence. Jillian could hear the wheels turning. "Plus, I figured I'd give you—the agency—a head start in controlling the situation before the police and media get their hands all over it. We have a dirty agent, Keller." She waited, then caught Sam's eye when the dead air stretched out. Sam rolled her hand. "I know it sounds crazy, but we've worked together for, how long? You know I'm not a murderer. Didn't you find it odd that Donaldson asked for me when he needed someone for a religion case? With my history?"

"Well, a little, but—I was shocked, you know, when they arrested you."

"Yeah, at work, in the garage. Do you know why I was there? Because Donaldson told me to come in, that the agency would help to clear the matter up. If I'd done it, do you think I'd have rolled into work that day? The media had already picked up the story. I was already out of town. I would have kept going."

"If you're innocent, why did you—forget it. I saw the evidence." He blew out some air. "Look, I help you, and I'm an accessory."

"That's—"

"Who broke you out?"

Jillian hesitated. "I'll tell you that part later. Look, I don't expect you to take what I'm saying on faith. I'm willing to give you some of the evidence I have on Donaldson. Take a look at it. If you find it interesting, get me a damn good lawyer who'll arrange what I want."

"You want us to meet?"

"No. Go out to your car."

"What?"

"Go out to your car."

"Shit, Jillian." Rustling.

"He's coming out," Bill murmured.

"Okay, I'm out here," Keller said. "Now what?"

"Pull down the visor on the driver's side."

Bill grunted. "He's getting into the car."

"Son of a bitch!" Keller breathed.

"It's to a locker in the downtown bus station," Jillian said. "Inside, you'll find an envelope. Trust me, once you see what's in it, you'll be on the phone to a lawyer, the police, and Director Hudson. I'll call you at nine tomorrow morning." She hung up. Her shoulders slumped, and her hand shook as she handed the phone back to Sam. If Keller didn't bite . . .

"There he goes," Bill said.

Jillian swallowed. "The evidence might not sway him."

"It will," Sam said firmly. "He's not going to get any sleep tonight. The police will be raiding Donaldson's other residence before the sun's up, I'm sure of it. You did good."

Would it really be over tomorrow? Her name cleared, her reputation restored—and her life never the same.

"Where to next? The safe house?" Bill asked.

Sam shook her head. "The airport. We're picking up Warren and a couple of rental cars," she said, catching Jillian's eye.

JILLIAN TRIED NOT to watch the clock as it crawled toward nine a.m. The cereal she'd had for breakfast sat in a lump in her stomach. If Keller didn't come through, she'd die an accused murderer, with her escape having convicted her in the court of public opinion. *8:59.*

Sam strode into the kitchen. "I bet he's chomping at the bit to hear from you."

Jillian hoped so.

Sam handed her the phone. "Go."

Bracing herself, she brought up Keller's number and called him. He picked up on the first ring. "Jillian?"

"Yes."

"They're ready. Your papers."

Her spirit soared. "My immunity papers?"

"Yeah, and all charges will be dropped." He paused. "I can't believe it. Donaldson and Preston in it together, and that bastard setting you up. Jesus."

"Yeah, I was the intended fall guy all along. There was no case."

"The police want the rest of it."

"They'll get it."

"They'll want to know who the hell broke you out and where you've been."

She'd spin them a good yarn. "Where do you want to meet?"

"The detectives want to speak with you. How about we meet at the downtown station at ten?"

She mouthed Keller's suggestion to Sam, who nodded. "Sure. The lawyer will be there, right?" Since the immunity papers were ready, Keller must have engaged one.

"Yeah, she'll be with me."

"Her name isn't Trotter, is it?"

"No, why?"

"Never mind. See you at ten." She hung up. "I hope I'm not walking into another trap."

"You won't be. Warren called me half an hour ago. The police searched Donaldson's house around five this morning."

Great! While she'd sat here trying not to throw up her cereal, Sam had known the plan was working. "I might have wanted to know about that earlier," Jillian drawled, controlling her irritation with difficulty. Was Sam getting back at her?

Sam held up her hand. "I would have told you, but Roberta called me right afterward and I just got off the phone with her—and Jeremy. We have things to arrange, and not a lot of time to do it."

"I know." Damn it! "I'm sorry. I'm sounding like a spoiled child."

Sam's face softened. "It's been one heck of a roller coaster ride for you."

Still. She'd made her decision, was at peace with it, and couldn't have everything her own way. If anyone was under stress now, it was Sam. "I didn't realize Warren isn't here."

"He left around one, figuring he might as well get into his routine. I bet he's snoring away in a hotel right now." She stood. "Let's get going. Traffic's still busy at this time. We don't want to be late."

WHEN SAM PULLED up to the curb around the corner from the police station, Jillian took her time unfastening her seatbelt. She wouldn't have minded the traffic delaying them for a few more minutes. It would be weird to leave the car, walk away, and not see Sam in her peripheral vision. She rested her hand on the door handle and turned to her.

"Sam . . ."

Sam continued to stare out the windshield. "Go, before I change my mind and drag you back to the island."

Determined not to behave like a spoiled child again, Jillian reluctantly opened the door and climbed out onto the sidewalk. Damn, she should have slipped a thank you note into Sam's book! Why did she always think of the ideal thing to say *after* a conversation, and the ideal thing to do when she was no longer in a position to do it?

As she rounded the corner, she couldn't help glancing at the car. Knowing Sam was still there calmed her rising jitters. She was delivering herself into the hands of the police, who wouldn't have thought twice about shooting her, this time yesterday.

Her heart pounding, she walked up the path that led to the station and pulled open the glass door. Relief washed over her when Keller leaped up from one of the chairs lining the reception area. He pointed at her head. "If I didn't know you were coming, the new look might have fooled me."

She touched her hair. "I'll be glad to go back to being a brunette."

A middle-aged woman in a blue business suit, a satchel slung over her shoulder, appeared at Keller's elbow. Keller gestured toward Jillian. "This is Jillian Campbell. Jillian, this is Jean Porter, the best damn lawyer we have at the agency."

This was the type of treatment she'd expected when she'd driven right into Donaldson's trap. "Pleased to meet you." She stuck out her hand.

Porter smiled and shook it. "Officer," she barked, "we need a room."

The officer behind the counter stuck his thumb over his shoulder. "Room thirty is free."

"When the prosecutor for the Donaldson case arrives, tell him where we are. See you in a bit," she said to Keller, then motioned for Jillian to follow her.

They'd only just settled themselves into the seats on one side of a rectangular table when two men and a woman entered. Jillian wished she and Porter hadn't sat; they were at a disadvantage. But, eager to get down to business, the three newcomers pulled out their chairs and introduced themselves. Everyone fidgeted and tried not to make eye contact while the prosecutor, the shorter of the two men, went through the paperwork with Porter.

Jillian's heart leaped into her mouth when Porter said, "I'd like to discuss this with my client. In private."

Hoping there wasn't a problem, Jillian fought the urge to snatch the paperwork away from Porter. It seemed to take forever for the prosecutor and the two detectives to file from the room and close the door behind them. "What is it?" she blurted.

"It's okay," Porter said, giving Jillian's arm a reassuring pat. "Everything's in order, but I want to go through it with you."

Jillian listened as Porter discussed each document page by page, summarizing the key points. All existing charges dropped, no new charges would be laid related to her escape, immunity from any further prosecution related to Jim and Joanna's murders or Donaldson's case. "Of course, you will be expected to testify at Donaldson's trial," Porter said.

"I'll do whatever I can to help. If I hadn't been framed, I would have been first in line to help the police in their investigation into

Jim and Joanna's deaths."

Satisfied, Porter nodded. "I could use a coffee before we get into it with them. Do you want anything?"

"A tea would be nice." Wait. "What about my personal effects?" She had no money or ID. "And what happened to my car?"

"You're not a free woman yet," Porter said, her eyes dancing with amusement. "They'll have everything for you at the desk when you leave. As for your car . . . I don't know what shape it's in. I'll look into it for you."

"Thanks."

Porter swung the door open and beckoned to someone in the corridor. An officer stepped into the room. Yeah, she wasn't a free woman yet.

Ten minutes later, everyone had reassembled. When Porter pressed a pen into her hand, Jillian hoped it wouldn't shake as she signed her name. The documents were passed back and forth across the table. Jillian scribbled her signature for the final time, rested the pen on the table, and gulped down some tea.

"I believe you promised us something," Detective Goldman said.

"There's a package in a locker at the bus station," she said, not sure whether Goldman knew about the package Keller had picked up. "I left the key with a friend. She'll give it to Keller."

Weiss, the female detective, slipped from the room and returned with Keller a minute later.

"Can I borrow someone's phone to call her?" Jillian said. Porter offered hers. Jillian punched in the number she'd memorized.

"Yeah," Sam said.

"I just signed all the paperwork."

"Congratulations."

"Keller's on his way for the key."

"Okay."

"Sam," Jillian quickly said.

"What?"

Tears welled in her eyes. Aware of everyone watching and listening, she blinked them back and struggled to keep them out of her voice. "You could have turned me away, but you didn't. Thanks for helping me."

Silence, then, "You're welcome." The line went dead.

Jesus, get a grip on yourself. She cleared her throat and handed the phone back to Porter. "Light blue sedan around the corner. She's wearing a gray hoodie."

"Does she know what's in the package?" Weiss asked. "Was she involved in your escape?"

"No. I called her this morning and asked her to help me out. All she knows is that I agreed to come in and make a deal, and to give the key to Keller."

"I'll be waiting in reception," Weiss said to Keller. "Bring it right back." She shifted her attention to Goldman. "Shouldn't take me long to check it out. I'll call you."

Goldman nodded. "I'll be back," he murmured to Jillian and Porter.

"Since my business is concluded, I'll leave you to it." The prosecutor stood and offered Jillian his hand. "Thank you, Ms. Campbell. I'll be in touch about testifying at Donaldson's trial." He left with Goldman.

Porter turned to Jillian. "Once Weiss confirms that the package strengthens their case, you'll be free to go, but I think Detective Goldman has questions."

"Sure. Like I said, I want to help." Plus, in here, Jillian felt safe. Out there . . . She had to leave the station sometime.

"I should call my office," Porter said, rising. "I'll be back in time for Goldman."

Jillian nodded. She'd rather sit alone too, than in awkward silence. This time they locked her in the room. She was on camera, no doubt. Someone was watching the riveting images of her sipping tea. She crossed her legs and waited. The bus station wasn't far away, so it wouldn't take long for Weiss to confirm that Jillian had upheld her part of the bargain.

Sure enough, Goldman and Porter returned fifteen minutes later. "You're a free woman, Ms. Campbell." Goldman gripped the back of a chair and tossed a notepad onto the table. "But I'd like to ask you some questions." When Jillian nodded, he pulled out the chair and sat. "Let's start with where you've been for the past week."

AN HOUR LATER, Jillian forced a smile when Goldman picked up his notebook and slipped his pen into his pocket. Thank god it was over, and for the papers she'd signed. She didn't know whether Goldman believed her tale about Jim Preston's powerful friends who'd known she was innocent, and that Donaldson, who'd caused problems for Jim, had committed the murders. Jim would have been horrified if Donaldson had successfully framed Jillian, a woman Jim had come to respect while working with her at the community centre. Worried that Jim's enemies might kill Jillian in prison, his friends had felt compelled to break her out and set the record straight. Honour among thieves, and all that.

No, she didn't know their full names, hadn't asked them to rescue her, didn't know where she'd stayed, and hadn't ventured outside before today. The policeman who thought he'd spotted her had been mistaken. Jim's friends had uncovered Donaldson's treachery and treated her well; apart from acknowledging that they'd committed a crime by snatching her from police custody, she couldn't fault them. In fact, she was grateful to them. After she'd called Keller this morning, they'd blindfolded her and dropped her off at a bus stop with a bus token, a few dollars, and the locker key. She'd borrowed someone's phone and called her friend, who'd picked her up and driven her here.

Yes, she'd testify against Donaldson and divulge everything she knew about Jim Preston and his associate. No, if the police arrested those who'd aided her over the past week—good luck with that—she wouldn't testify against them. Without their help, she'd be in prison, and Donaldson would be enjoying the spoils from his criminal activities.

Goldman hadn't liked her protective attitude toward her "hosts," but tough. As Porter had reminded him, they weren't part of the deal.

"Where can I reach you?" Goldman asked.

Jillian gave him her work number. Then he was gone. Porter grinned and picked up her satchel.

"Thank you," Jillian said.

"Thank your boss. He dragged me out of bed at 11:30 last night and made sure the ball kept rolling." She walked with Jillian to the reception area.

Jillian's heart sank when she spotted a group of reporters and cameramen through the window. "Someone must have tipped them off," a male voice said to her right.

She turned. Keller was still here? He must feel guilty about not lifting a finger to help her when she was arrested.

"The police picked up Donaldson at the airport half an hour ago." Keller's lip curled. "From hotel food to prison food. The bastard deserves it. I feel sorry for the wife and kids, though."

And the mistress, poor thing.

"You going home?"

She grimaced. "No. I'm not stepping back into that apartment again, not after Donaldson had his mitts all over everything. You saw the evidence."

Keller bit his lip. "Yeah."

Blood rushed to her cheeks. That damn semen report! "It didn't happen."

"I know. I mean, I never . . ." His Adam's apple bobbed.

"I'm going to my mother's," she said, deciding to rescue him. He may have initially looked the other way, but then he'd come through for her, big time. "I have a visit to finish. When I'm back in town, I'll stay in a hotel until I find a new place."

"Speaking about coming back into town . . . you need time off, for sure, but . . . well, how much time? When do you think you'll be ready to come back to work?"

"I don't know, Keller. Can I go back to work? My face has been all over the news."

"So you can't go undercover for a year or two. So what? You'll work cases that don't require it."

She shook her head. "To be honest, I'm wondering whether the agency is still for me."

"What?" he bleated, his eyes bulging.

She brushed a stray hair out of her eye. "I had a lot of time to think about my life over the past week."

"Sure, while you were trying to prove your innocence. Come on, now's not the time to make serious decisions. You might not be thinking clearly."

She inwardly snorted. She was thinking clearer than she had in years.

Someone tapped her on the shoulder. "Jillian, they have your things," Porter said, jutting her chin toward the counter.

"Is there a car rental place around here?" Jillian asked.

"Let me get my car," Keller said. "I'll bring it round to the front, so you don't have to walk to the parking lot with the bunch out there chasing you. I'll take you to the nearest car rental."

"Thanks." She put her hand on his arm. "For everything. If you hadn't stuck your neck out and gone to the locker, I don't know what I would have done."

He roughly patted her hand. "I'm glad I helped make it right."

She went to the counter with Porter and collected personal items that felt as if they belonged to someone else. She pulled on her watch, slipped the birthstone ring onto her finger—topaz, a birthday gift from Mom and Danny one year. Her wallet was there, but not her phone or satchel; she'd have to act as if she cared and try to track them down. Her agency ID . . . Jillian gazed at her photo. The person smiling back at her—the imposter, the role-player, the one afraid to live—no longer existed. She'd grown up, aged years over the past week.

She slid the ID card into her back pocket and peered into the paper bag the officer had plunked onto the counter with her other effects. The clothes she was wearing when she was arrested were here, but not the ones they'd taken from Mom's. She'd have to go shopping.

"Ready to run the gauntlet?" Porter asked as Jillian rolled the bag shut.

Butterflies took flight in her stomach. She smiled wanly and nodded. They walked to the glass doors. The hubbub began the moment her feet hit the path outside.

"Jillian, how does it feel to be exonerated?"

"Ms. Campbell, over here!"

Reporters pressed in from both sides. She held the bag in front of her face, lowered her head, and followed the path, her skin crawling. A Beguiler could easily blend into the mob and slip a knife between her ribs.

"Ms. Campbell won't be making a statement today," Porter shouted, motioning for a cameraman to get out of her way.

"Jillian, where were you hiding out the past week?"

"Marcy Abrams of News World Five. Come onto our show. Tell your story!"

"Will you sue the police?"

"Be on your guard, Jillian."

She jerked her head up. *Sam.* Jillian searched for her, but all she saw were microphones, cameras, recorders, reporters jostling for position.

They'd reached the car. Porter spun around, raised her arms, and started to speak, drawing the attention of most of the reporters while Jillian yanked the passenger door open and fell into the car. The moment she pulled the door shut, Keller stepped on the accelerator. He suddenly braked and honked his horn. "Jesus, did you see that?" he shouted, gesturing at the windshield. "The idiot stepped right in front of the car. Anything for a story, for Christ's sake."

The cameraman jumped back onto the sidewalk. Jillian pushed away from the dashboard and reached for her seatbelt. The mob and the police station shrank in the side-view mirror.

She was free.

Chapter Seventeen

Jillian pulled into Mom's driveway, turned off the engine, and gazed out the windshield. Maybe coming here was a bad idea. Endangering herself was one thing; endangering Mom and Danny was selfish. Sam had figured it would take the Beguilers at least a few days to regroup. What if she was wrong? Jillian's encounter with Lilibeth had taught her a harsh lesson. They'd be cruel. They'd take great pleasure in making her watch Mom and Danny beg for their deaths. She should have listened to Sam and gone along with what she wanted. But it was too late now; the front door had opened. Jillian forced a smile and met Mom at the bottom of the steps.

"Oh my god, honey," Mom cried. They awkwardly hugged. "I couldn't believe it when you called and said they'd dropped the charges."

Jillian bit back the retort that instantly sprang to her tongue. Mom hadn't meant that she'd doubted her innocence.

Danny waited in the foyer. His embrace felt warmer. "What happened? Where have you been?"

She let out a long, heartfelt sigh. "To be honest, I need a tea and something to eat. Then I'll tell you everything." Or, rather, a more censored version of what she'd told Goldman.

"Are you really free? All charges dropped?"

"On the news, they said they'd arrested some man that works for the government," Mom said.

This was it, the point of no return. "I work for the government, Mom. I know I've always said I work for a bank, but I've been lying.

I wasn't allowed to tell you what I really do. Given everything that's happened, though, my boss told me I could tell you, so I can explain how I ended up accused of murder. You can't tell anyone, though."

Mom and Danny stared at her, and not because of her hair colour—she'd warned them about that on the phone. She could read the question in their eyes: how well did they know her? She'd only seen them a couple of times a year, but that didn't matter. Apart from her real occupation, there wasn't much to know. They knew her as well as anyone did—except for the Fellowship. Well, in the time she had left with Mom and Danny, she'd try to make up for it. Omissions, yes. There was no point in coming out to them, and she'd gloss over many details regarding the events of the past week. But no more outright lies—the one she'd just told them about having permission to divulge her real job would be her last. "Donaldson, the man they arrested . . . I was working on a case for him. That's how I got mixed up in everything. I'll tell you all about it after I've had something to eat."

"Let me go fix you a sandwich," Danny said.

"I can do it."

"No, let me. You look like you need to sit down." He lifted a brow. "You haven't lied about peanut butter, have you?"

Relieved to see the mischievous glint in his eyes, she shook her head. "I really can't stand the stuff."

"Then it'll be ham."

Mom played with the chain around her neck and strode into the living room. "How long will you be staying?"

"A couple of days. I wanted to finish my visit," Jillian said, trying to inject levity into her voice.

Mom walked to the window and peered through the sheer curtain. "That's not your car."

Jillian went to her side. "It's a rental. The police still have mine." Her eyes swept the road outside, the sidewalk, the yards across the street. Never again would she gaze innocently out this window.

JILLIAN SIGNED HER name on the line, then watched as Evans and his assistant signed as witnesses. "And we're done," Evans said as he put his pen down. "I'll keep the original on file here. Would you like a copy?"

"Yes, please."

The assistant gathered up the pages and bustled from the room. Jillian leaned back in her chair. When she'd called yesterday to make the appointment, the secretary had balked, until Jillian had mentioned her name. Apparently she'd become something of a quasi-celebrity. Suddenly Evans had room in his schedule for the following afternoon. "Thank you for taking me on such short notice."

Evans clasped his hands on top of his desk. "Think nothing of it. These days, with computers and templates, it doesn't take long for Nancy to prepare a document, especially for simple wills like yours."

"I'd put it off much too long. The past week got me thinking . . ."

Evans nodded sagely. "Some people feel a bit weird about doing their will. They think it's morbid. But it's better to dictate what you want, rather than to leave it up to the state." He cleared his throat. "The last week must have been quite the ordeal for you."

Jillian grimaced. "Yes. It's still too fresh to talk about."

"I understand," he said quickly.

They sat in awkward silence, listening to the sound of the photocopy machine working its magic. Jillian mentally counted the pages. Amazing how a lawyer could produce five pages from, "Leave everything to Mom and Danny, and make Danny the executor."

Finally the assistant returned. Evans inspected the copy, then slipped it into a manila envelope, along with a handful of business cards. "Make sure to give one to your parents," he said.

After paying for professional services rendered, Jillian left Evans' office and rode the elevator down to the lobby. She paused near the exit, slid the will from the envelope, and read the title page. *Last Will and Testament of Jillian Elizabeth Campbell*. Jesus.

Someone bumped her shoulder as he brushed by her, pushing her forward a step. "Sorry," he murmured without a backward glance. Her heart racing, she shoved the will back into the envelope. *Calm down.* The lobby was busy. He was just a man who hadn't watched where he was going. She inhaled deeply, exhaled slowly. Now what? This morning, Dad's grave had weighed on her mind. Not having visited it since moving away from home, she'd planned to drive to the cemetery after the appointment with Evans. But it was a two-hour drive each way, and Dad wasn't there. Jillian wanted to spend her remaining time with the living, not the dead. She left the building and self-consciously walked through the parking lot.

Ten minutes later, she strolled up Mom's front path. Danny sat in his habitual chair on the porch. He rested his book on his lap when Jillian sank into the wooden chair next to his. "Beautiful day," she said.

"Yes, it is."

One of the kids from across the street rode by on his bike. The dog next door chased after him but quickly gave up and ran back to its yard, its tail wagging. "Danny, I need to tell you something."

He turned to her. "What is it?"

"When you first met Mom, started dating her, I know I was difficult." She snorted. "Okay, I'm surprised I didn't scare you away, and damn grateful. You're the best thing that ever happened to Mom. It's been easier for me, knowing you're here with her, and that you'll always take care of her. I know I've been distant, but I love both of you." Her fingers dug into her skin through her jeans. She squinted out at the street. She wouldn't cry. She would not cry. "I'm sorry I gave you such a hard time."

"Jillian." She felt his hand on her arm. "I understood why you weren't happy with my sudden appearance in your life. The last thing you wanted was another father. And after what happened with your father, you were afraid for your mother. I understood that."

"Still—"

"You were fifteen. I was the adult. And you weren't as bad as you think you were—or maybe you were, but I loved you too much to take much notice. Because I fell in love with both my girls. Still crazy about your mother. Still proud of my stepdaughter."

She blinked and bit her lip. *Hold it together!*

"What aren't you telling us, sweetheart?" Danny said softly.

"What do you mean?"

"You seem different . . . more comfortable with yourself. There's a calmness about you. It reminds me of a friend who died of cancer. When the chemo wasn't helping, he raged about it, then cried about it, then vowed to fight it. I thought he'd go out still insisting he'd beat it, but I visited the week before he died, and he was calm. He'd accepted it. He'd found his peace." Danny was silent for a moment. "Are you ill?"

"No." She clenched her hands in front of her. "I had a lot of time to think over the past week. I was faced with having my life ripped away from me. I thought about all the things I wished I'd said to people . . . all the things I wish I'd done." She brightened. "In fact, I think I'll take up the guitar again."

"The guitar?" Danny guffawed. "I remember you in front of the mirror in your bedroom, jumping up and down, doing your fancy guitar moves and wailing your heart out." His belly shook. "Your singing frightened me more than your shouting did."

"Well, thank you very much," she said, chuckling. "Notice I didn't say I'd take up singing. There's a reason for that."

Danny's amusement faded first. "Are you sure that's all it is? Facing life in prison made you evaluate your life?"

No, until arriving at the courthouse, she'd still been telling herself that the police would realize they'd made a terrible mistake. It was her time with Sam that had turned her world upside down, but Keller calling her in to see Donaldson had been the catalyst. Sam's voice echoed through her mind: *You lost your life the moment you walked into the community centre that first time.* Funny, Jillian now viewed that event as the first step in reclaiming her life—but she understood what Sam had meant, and that it was true. "That's all it is," she said to Danny. Another lie of omission, but only in the details.

They both jumped when the screen door flew open. Mom stepped onto the porch. "Come quick!" she shrieked, motioning to them. "It's on the news."

Jillian followed Mom into the house with Danny on her heels. On the TV, Chief Williams was addressing a gaggle of reporters. ". . . autopsy will take place later today," he was saying.

"Did he have any visible injuries?" a reporter asked.

"The autopsy report will address that," Williams said.

"Was it suicide?"

"We can't rule out anything at this time."

"Marcy Abrams from News World Five. When was he last seen alive?"

"All I can say is that Mr. Donaldson died sometime after eleven p.m."

Jillian sank onto the sofa. Donaldson was dead? How? Had the Beguilers gotten to him? Had they regrouped already? She could be next. Wait—or was it the Fellowship? Donaldson dead, case closed, evidence not scrutinized. Or maybe the coward had killed himself, or had a heart attack.

"You all right, honey?" Mom asked. "You look a bit pale."

She nodded and wiped her brow with an unsteady hand. "It means I won't have to testify."

"That's good," Danny said, fortunately, focused on the TV.

She heard Sam's voice again: *"I operate at a different level than everyone else. I move in a world most people don't know exists, in which man's law doesn't mean a thing."* In which one could no longer naively watch the news; in which threats lurked around every corner.

JILLIAN WALKED INTO the kitchen and glanced at the time on the microwave: *6:55.* Mom placed the last dish into the dishwasher and swung its door shut. Perhaps sensing Jillian, she turned around. Since waking that morning, Jillian had thought about what she'd say to Mom that wouldn't upset her. She'd had plenty of opportunity to talk to her alone. They'd gone shopping together before lunch and had spent most of the afternoon in front of the TV, watching the talk and reality shows Mom enjoyed. But Jillian's indecision about what to say had paralyzed her. What did she want to say?

I never appreciated how difficult it must have been for you after Dad died. A disgraced dead husband; single mother to a confused and devastated daughter; the looks; the whispers. Her and Mom's distant relationship, with neither knowing how to bridge the gap. Did Mom see Dad when she looked at her daughter? Had she known the full extent of Dad's betrayal? Did it matter at this point?

I'm sorry I haven't visited very often. And felt guilty for all the times she'd thought of driving up the highway, but instead killed time watching TV or reading, while counting down the hours until she'd no longer be Jillian Campbell. She'd looked down her nose at Mom's TV habit. Pot, kettle, black. If only they could have reached out to each other, rather than spending their time living vicariously through strangers.

I'm so sorry for the pain I'm going to cause you. Because despite their strained relationship and their inability to emotionally connect with each other, Mom loved her, and she loved Mom. *You're strong, Mom. You're a survivor.* And this time, she'd have Danny.

I love you. That was what she wanted to say, but in a way that wouldn't make this conversation a horribly awkward one.

Jillian met Mom's eyes. "The casserole was delicious. Man, I wish I was half the cook you are. And I've really enjoyed being here. I always do, but this time . . . being with people I feel safe with and trust . . . it's meant everything. I know I haven't been the most attentive daughter, but you and Danny . . ." Shit, shit, shit, she was starting to lose it. Deep breath . . .

Mom's hand went to her hip. "You know you're always welcome here, honey. Do you want the recipe?"

"What?"

"The recipe. For the casserole."

She shook herself. "Yeah, sure."

"I'll copy it for—oh, wait. It's almost seven! You'll stay and watch my favourite show with me, right?" She walked to Jillian, threw her arm around her shoulders, and gave her a quick squeeze.

"Yeah, I said I'd head out around 8:30."

Mom smiled. "Good. I'll copy the recipe out for you after the show, then." She turned the dishwasher on and grasped Jillian's arm. "Come on. It'll be fun watching it with you. I can't think of anyone else I'd rather watch it with."

Jillian's throat tightened. *I love you, too.*

JILLIAN ZIPPED HER bag shut, slung it over her shoulder, and took one last look around the guest room. Part of her wished she could stay another day or two; the other part knew that every extra hour she remained would potentially put Mom and Danny in harm's way. It was time to go. She pulled the door open and walked down the hallway, deliberately dropping one of Evans' business cards to the hardwood floor. He'd probably contact them, but leaving a card for Mom to find wouldn't hurt. She'd assume Jillian had dropped it, add it to the pile she kept in a drawer, and hopefully remember it after the police had left and the initial shock had passed.

When Jillian reached the foyer, Mom and Danny emerged from the living room. Mom glanced at the bag Jillian dropped to the floor. "Ready to go?"

Jillian nodded.

"I heard you talking to someone on the phone," Mom said, failing to mask her curiosity.

"I was just letting a friend know that I'm leaving. A female friend," she quickly added when Mom's eyes lit up. Mom had stopped asking about boyfriends years ago, but still clung to the hope that Jillian would settle down with a nice man and have 1.6 children. It wasn't to be.

"Are you sure you have to leave tonight?" Danny asked. "You look tired."

"Leave tomorrow after breakfast," Mom said.

"I can't. I need to go home. It's time for me to go home." Normally she'd open the door to avoid the awkward "should we hug?" moment, but tonight she reached for Danny and held him tighter than she usually did, then she hugged Mom with the abandon of her ten-year-old self, and brushed her lips against Mom's cheek. The moment she let Mom go, she turned away and picked up the bag. "Take care," she said, before her throat grew too thick with tears to speak. She waved without looking over her shoulder. Her face already trembled. Thank god it was dark.

She cursed under her breath as she fumbled with the rental car key, and finally managed to unlock the damn door. She almost tossed her bag into the backseat, but stopped herself just in time and set it on the passenger seat. Mom and Danny stood silhouetted in the doorway. She reversed out of the driveway, then slowly cruised by the house and returned their waves, relieved that they couldn't see her wet cheeks. Then they were gone.

Good-bye.

BREAKING NEWS: Another twist tonight in the Jim Preston double murder case. Jillian Campbell, the woman accused and then exonerated in the murders of Preston and his associate, was killed in an accident on rural Highway 22 when her car veered into oncoming traffic and collided with a tractor trailer. According to police,

Campbell's car burst into flames upon impact. She died instantly. In what one paramedic called a miracle, the driver of the tractor trailer escaped with only minor injuries and was treated at the scene.

Donald Donaldson, the accused in the Preston case, was found dead in his cell yesterday morning. When asked whether Campbell's and Donaldson's deaths are related, Chief Williams said that there's no evidence to suggest a connection between the two events.

Campbell was thirty-six years old. She leaves behind her mother and stepfather.

Other titles by Sarah Ettritch

Threaded Through Time
The Salbine Sisters
The Missing Comatose Woman
The Rymellan Series

If you'd like to be notified when Sarah releases a new book, sign up
for the notification list at www.sarahettritch.com.

Thanks for reading!

www.ingramcontent.com/pod-product-compliance
Lightning Source LLC
Chambersburg PA
CBHW031246210726
48287CB00003B/914

ONE

"Pieces of eight, ya old bats."

Alexandra Meyers, a.k.a. Xandie, Librarian to the Supernatural Great Library of Alexandria, dropped flat on the dusty wooden floor as the red and blue kamikaze parrot dive-bombed her head. "This is not what I expected when Elspeth promised us an all-expenses-paid weekend away."

Lila Harrow, cousin to Xandie and baker witch extraordinaire, shook her head, disgusted. "And you trusted her? Have you dipped into Theo's catnip stash?"

"I should have. Might make this weekend easier to deal with." Xandie's cat, Theo, had been a porn-scroll-reading, hipflask-guzzling, ancient Greek teenager. Thanks to a demon-possessed Julius Caesar burning the physical Great Library down, he'd turned into an immortal black feline guardian. And a pain in Xandie's well-padded tush.

Holly, another Harrow cousin, reached out a hand and hoisted Xandie to her feet. "I'm sure Elspeth can help you out with any illegal medicinal aids you need."

"I'm staying as far away as I can manage from that chaos-loving fibber. *Free weekend my...*"

Holly clapped a hand over Xandie's mouth. "Elspeth, we were just coming to update you on the bird situation."

Elspeth Harrow, matriarch of the Harrow clan, narrowed her amber eyes and glared at her granddaughters. "If you're going to lie, banshee, at least do it with skill. Your nose twitches every time. It's a bad tell. Never sit at my poker table. On the other hand..." Elspeth toyed with a corkscrew curl from her turquoise-colored wig. "You should sit in on a game or two. It'd be like taking candy from a baby."

"Haven't you already done that? I'm sure we had a whole bowl of leftover Halloween candy. Now it's all gone." Winifred, Elspeth's youngest daughter, joined the group.

"My payment for annoying me with your Halloween antics. Whoever heard of a witch riding a broom?" Elspeth curled her lip at the idea. "Now where is the putrid parrot? Colin refuses to come down and socialize while that winged menace stalks him."

"Coward. Coward," Petunia squawked from a high beam on the roof, out of reach of the women.

All the Harrow witches, including Xandie, narrowed the same amber eyes at the taunting avian. Xandie pasted a welcoming smile on her face and extended a fist. "Why don't you come down here, Petunia? See what I have for you?"

Petunia cocked her head to the side and considered the offering. She gathered herself and launched into the air, swooping low above the women.

Xandie grabbed at the bird but missed by a finger length.

"Petunia no dummy," the bird squawked again and disappeared from sight.

Xandie shook the same fist in the air, cursing the too-smart bird.

"Seriously? You tried trapping a piratical parrot with air and a fake-out?" Holly shook her smooth chin-length brown bob in fake shame.

All the cousins had a similar shade of dark brown hair. Holly, the youngest, had a slim build and a quiet nature. She preferred to think before acting, unlike drama llama Lila. A banshee witch hybrid, Holly had an affinity for death and a link to the Harrow family. Whenever there was the possibility of a death in or around the family, Holly wailed banshee style. Silver eyes and prophetic visions of death. And in the case of the original wicked witch, Elspeth, this happened almost daily.

Xandie focused on her dismissive cousin. "You try catching the cursed feathered freak. It loves tormenting me."

Holly nibbled her lip, thinking Xandie's words over. "Deal. I'll catch Petunia, and you owe me a favor. No expiration date, right?"

Let her banshee cousin try running after the parrot for a while. "Fine."

The girls shook hands with Holly looking satisfied and Xandie relieved.

"She suckered you, Xandie. Holly has a bunch of this seed stuff she mistakenly calls a snack. She'll have painful Petunia eating out of her hand, literally, in minutes."

Tall and curvy Lila, the eldest of the grandchildren by two weeks, had luxurious curly brown locks and the same eyes as the rest of her family. Lila poured heart and soul and witchy Harrow gifts into her baking. Pick a treat from her bakery and top up on positive vibes and self-confidence. On the other hand, whenever she was upset or angry, it was best to stay away from Lila's baked goods. Xandie shuddered at the memory of the spoiled pastries and food fight incidents from the past.

"Whatever you do, I don't care, but keep that parrot away from my baby, Colin."

"They will. They know how much Colin means to you," Winifred soothed her mother, her plump cheeks wobbling as she glared at her daughter and nieces.

"If no one has anything to do, I have a task." The housekeeper, a no-nonsense middle-aged woman with auburn hair slicked back into a bun pursed her lips. She singled out Xandie with a pointed, red-tipped nail. "You. You definitely have strong muscles."

Xandie tapped her chest. "Me?" Surely the woman had looked at her sugar-loving waistline? Strong wasn't a word she'd use to describe her curves and addiction to all things sweet.

"Yes, you. Oue guest here..." She pointed to Elspeth. "... left a bag at the dock. I need you to pick it up and bring it to the main house." She clapped her hands. "Hop to it."

Elspeth poked her tongue out at her granddaughter and crossed her eyes, mentally daring Xandie to lose it.

The old bag reveled in chaos and Xandie refused to aid and abet her elderly and slightly evil grandmother. "Fine." She bit the word out and spun on the spot before trudging outside.

Hedgewater Manor had an old English vibe going on, with red bricks, gables, and the odd gargoyle. Multiple levels of ostentatious bricks and the crowning glory, a looming widow's walk.

Xandie shuddered as she stomped down the driveway and veered off onto a small path which led to the boathouse and a private dock. "More like a Scooby Doo haunted mansion. I expect hidden passageways and eyes watching me from the paintings." She picked her way down the path to the dock, passing a paint-peeling boathouse with pretty white shutters.

"I'm doing my best," she grumbled. "It won't be as easy as Elspeth thinks to keep an eye on the Hedgewaters. There probably *are* hidden passages everywhere." Her sleuthing nerve tingled. Hidden passageways sounded interesting. She took a step forward just as the boathouse door swung open, almost taking her out.

"Watch where you're going." A tall man with broad shoulders, ice-blue eyes, and a sneer in place glowered down at Xandie.

She stuck out a hand in greeting. "Sorry, the housekeeper told me a lost bag is hiding down here somewhere?"

The man ignored Xandie's hand, grabbed a bright pink bag from next to the door, and shoved it into her arms.

"Gee, thanks." Xandie settled the bag in her arms. "I'm Xandie. My grandmother volunteered me and my cousins to help this weekend." She waited for the grumpy bag-shover to introduce himself.

Relenting, he nodded at Xandie. "I'm David Riley, the caretaker here. If you need something, speak to the housekeeper or me." He crossed his arms and waited for Xandie to leave.

She smiled brightly. "You're young to be a caretaker. I always imagine a scary, grizzled old man when I hear that word."

David dragged a hand through shaggy brown hair. "My mother got me this job. I used to be in the army. I've only been here for a few months. Look, is there anything else I can do for you?"

Xandie stepped back and ran into someone coming up from the docks behind her.

"Watch yourself, you silly girl," a woman hissed and sidestepped Xandie.

"Sorry, I didn't realize you were behind me." Xandie hoisted Elapeth's pink bag higher in her arms. "I had to pick up a lost bag."

"Staff, I presume?" Without waiting for an answer, the woman waved at the dock. "Our bags are on the dock. The horrible ferry man wouldn't bring them up to the house. He expected us to lift our own bags." She shook her head in bemusement.

Xandie stared openmouthed at the blinged-out brassy blonde ordering her around like a servant.

"Now, Gloria, it doesn't hurt to be nice to staff." An elderly, skinny man with gray hair and pale blue eyes patted the woman on her bony shoulder. "This is my daughter-in-law, Gloria, and my two sons, Harrison and Herbert." He gestured to the two men standing behind him. "I'm Henry Hedgewater. My brother owns Sarah Island."

"Xandie Meyers. My grandmother, Elspeth, offered our help for the weekend."

"Aha, Elspeth Harrow." Henry slapped his skinny thigh in mirth. "Elspeth, entertaining to a fault. Of course, my brother hates her. But he loves the poker competition."

"That's Elspeth. Either love her or hate her."

Henry settled a companionable arm around Xandie's shoulder. "Look, sweetie. I'd consider it a personal favor if you made Gloria happy and hauled our bags up." He leaned closer and mock-whispered, "She's a bear when she's unhappy. Thankfully, I'm not married to her." He winked at Xandie and dropped his arm.

Gloria smirked at Xandie as she tottered past on ridicu-